The Chess Pla

Satyajit Ray is India's best-known film director. He first became known internationally for his Apu Trilogy, made in the 1950s. *The Chess Players* was made in 1977. Ray is also the author of many short stories and novellas for children in Bengali, some of which have been translated into European languages. He lives and works in Calcutta.

THE CHESS PLAYERS
and other screenplays

Edited by
ANDREW ROBINSON

faber and faber
LONDON · BOSTON

First published in 1989
by Faber and Faber Limited
3 Queen Square London WC1N 3AU

Phototypeset by Input Typesetting Ltd, London
Printed in Great Britain by
Richard Clay Limited Bungay Suffolk

British Library Cataloguing in Publication Data
is available.

ISBN 0-571-14074-2

CONTENTS

PREFACE

Of the three screenplays in this book, two – *The Chess Players* and *Deliverance* – are based on short stories by the famous Urdu and Hindi writer Prem Chand. The third, *The Alien*, is an original screenplay by me. The three subjects could hardly be more disparate in style and content. *Deliverance*, which was made for television, deals with Untouchability and is distinctly angry in tone. *The Chess Players*, which is about the annexation of an Indian native state by the British Raj, is quite often funny in spite of its weighty theme. It is also my most expensive film, whereas *Deliverance* cost very little money. *The Alien*, which was never filmed, is best described as a whimsy.

Three primary reasons drew me to *The Chess Players*: my interest in chess, in the Raj period, and in the city of Lucknow where I spent many delightful holidays in my childhood and youth. It is the capital of Oudh, which was annexed by the then Governor-General of India, Lord Dalhousie. This was done through the agency of General Outram, who was the British political agent in Lucknow. Research revealed that the deposed King Wajid Ali Shah was an extraordinary character. Outram describes him as a worthless king, which he probably was, but this was compensated for by a genuine gift for music. He was a composer, singer, poet and dancer. He also wrote and produced plays on Hindu themes (he was a Muslim himself) in which he acted the main part. All this made the King a figure worthy of film treatment. As for the character of Outram, I was struck by the fact that he had qualms about the task he had been assigned to perform. This was revealed in a couple of Dalhousie's letters. Thus both the King and Outram were complex, three-dimensional characters. Chess is used as a metaphor for the political manoeuvrings of the Raj as well as an actual ingredient of a subplot involving two noblemen addicts of the game. The two friends, fearing trouble, retire into a village and play right through the Annexation and the arrival of the British army in Lucknow. Their story is treated in a light vein, although there is a note of pathos at the end.

I made *Deliverance* because I had been wanting to make a film about the poorest of the poor, something I had never done before. The dramatic aspect of the Brahmin–Untouchable confrontation is vividly conveyed by Prem Chand in his story. I found it replete with cinematic possibilities.

The Alien germinated from a short story I wrote for the magazine for young people which I have been editing for the last twenty-five years. It concerned a meek village schoolmaster whose life is changed by an extraordinarily lucky encounter with an extraterrestrial. The idea of a supremely intelligent alien landing in a village where most of the inhabitants are unlettered lodged in my mind for a long time as a possible film subject. In 1966, I met Arthur Clarke on a visit to London. Kubrick had then been filming *2001* from Clarke's story, and Clarke had actually come to meet Kubrick. Clarke took me to the studio where I met the director and watched some of the shooting. On the way back from the studio, in the car, I gave Clarke a brief idea of the kind of sci-fi film I had in mind. Clarke encouraged me, and later, after his return to Sri Lanka where he lived, told his partner Mike Wilson about *The Alien*, which is the title I had in mind for my film. Wilson was enthused enough to fly down to Calcutta and make me write the screenplay virtually at the point of a gun. The work was completed in a fortnight. Wilson immediately started to work on setting up the production. Soon I found myself in Hollywood where Columbia had read the screenplay and had provisionally agreed to finance it. But, like many a cherished project, *The Alien* never really got off the ground.

The Alien was meant to be a bilingual film where the Indian characters would speak in Bengali among themselves, and all scenes involving the American engineer would be spoken in English. The screenplay, however, was written entirely in English. What is printed here is the first draft that Columbia found acceptable.

Satyajit Ray

THE CHESS PLAYERS

INTRODUCTION

The Chess Players, completed in 1977, was the first adult film about the British Raj in India. Today, after *Gandhi, Heat and Dust, The Jewel in the Crown, A Passage to India* and many other films, Ray's film remains by far the most sophisticated portrayal of this particular clash of cultures. No other director – British, Indian or otherwise – is likely to better it. As V. S. Naipaul remarked of it, 'It is like a Shakespeare scene. Only 300 words are spoken but goodness – terrific things happen.'

Satyajit Ray had known Prem Chand's short story *Shatranj ke Khilari* for more than thirty years before he attempted to make a screenplay out of it. Although it had first appeared in print in Hindi in the mid-1920s, Ray read it in English translation in the early 1940s as an art student at Rabindranath Tagore's university in Bengal and was immediately drawn to it for several reasons.

Lucknow, the setting of the story, is one of the most resonant cities of India. Satyajit took holidays there in the late 1920s and 1930s from the age of about eight, staying at first in the house of an uncle, later with other relatives. The uncle, a barrister called Atulprasad Sen, was the most famous Bengali composer of songs after Tagore. His house hummed with music of every kind, and his guests displayed polished manners to match; they included the greatest north Indian classical musician of modern times, Ustad Allauddin Khan (the father of Ali Akbar Khan and the guru of Ravi Shankar). The young Ray listened to him playing the piano and violin, and took in the atmosphere of courtly refinement which was so characteristic of Lucknow. He was also taken to see all the sights that had made Lucknow known as the 'Paris of the East' and the 'Babylon of India' a century before: the great mosque Bara Imambara with its notorious Bhulbhuliya Maze, the Dilkusha Garden, and the remains of the palaces of the Kings of Oudh. Nearby he saw the shell of the British Residency with the marks of Mutiny cannonballs still visible on its walls and a marble plaque commemorating the spot where Sir Henry Lawrence had fallen in 1857. Even today these places have a peculiar elegiac aura. The brief allusions to the city and that period in its history found in Prem Chand's story

3

conjured up a host of images and sensations in the twenty-year-old Ray's mind.

By then he was also keenly interested in chess. Over the next ten years or so this became an addiction – the main bond (along with western classical music) between him and his first English friend, an RAF serviceman with time on his hands in Calcutta in 1944–6, whose father happened to be a championship player. After this friend was demobbed, Ray found himself without a partner and took to playing solitaire chess. Over the next few years he became engrossed in it and bought books on the subject, which he would soon decide to sell to raise money to shoot pilot footage for his first film *Pather Panchali*. His passion for chess disappeared only with the onset of a greater passion: film-making.

That came around 1951, after his return to Calcutta from his first visit to Britain. Nearly a quarter of a century passed before Ray tackled the story he had admired as a student. His reluctance was principally due to his doubts about writing a screenplay and working with actors in a language – Urdu, the court language of Lucknow (which is very similar to Hindi, the language of Prem Chand's story) – not his own. So rich, subtle and life-like is Ray's usual film dialogue – as Naipaul has appreciated from just the portions of *The Chess Players* in English – so nuanced his direction of actors that he feared to work in a language other than Bengali or perhaps English. It was his affection for the story, his discovery of able Urdu collaborators, and his awareness of a pool of Urdu-speaking talent among actors in Bombay (rather than in his usual Calcutta), that eventually gave him confidence. For the first time, (barring *The Alien* and his documentaries), Ray wrote a screenplay in English, which was subsequently translated into Urdu. During production he spoke English to the actors and to his Urdu collaborators. Though his Hindi – which is technically India's national language – is serviceable, Ray characteristically avoids speaking it. 'He doesn't like to do anything unless he's really good at it,' Shama Zaidi, his chief collaborator in the writing of the screenplay has remarked.

Her role in the film began early on, about two years before Ray completed the first draft of the screenplay in June 1976. Ray's Art Director Bansi Chandragupta introduced her to Ray in 1974. He was just beginning to get to grips with his research for the film then – which makes it one of the longest preproduction periods of any Ray film (during which he made another film, *The Middle Man*). It is not hard to see why: not only had Ray taken on the re-creation of an entire culture not his own, he was also having to confront his own ambivalence towards the British Raj and, in particular, the contradictions of King Wajid Ali Shah, one of the most bizarre monarchs in a land of eccentric rulers.

Since Ray has regularly been condemned for failing to make his own attitude to the Indian or British side clear in *The Chess Players* – notably in a long attack on the film for accepting the British view of Wajid Ali Shah as being 'effete and effeminate', published in the *Illustrated Weekly of India*, to which Ray replied at length – it is worth detailing the principal sources he consulted in his research in India and, later, in the India Office Library in London. He listed them in his reply, adding his own comments on their significance, which are reproduced here along with my own remarks in square brackets:

1. *Blue Book on Oude*. This is the official British dossier on the Annexation. It contains, among other things, a verbatim account of Outram's last interview with Wajid, and describes Wajid's taking off his turban and handing it to Outram as a parting gesture.

2. Abdul Halim Sharar's *Guzeshta Lucknow* (translated into English by E. S. Harcourt and Fakhir Hussain as *Lucknow: The Last Phase of an Oriental Culture*). Sharar was born three years after Wajid's deposition [in 1856]. His father had worked in the Secretariat of Wajid's Court and joined Wajid [in exile in Calcutta] in 1862. Sharar went and joined his father seven years later. Introducing the book, the translators say:
   'The work has long been recognized by Indo–Islamic scholars as a primary source of great value, a unique document both alive and authentic in every detail.' Sharar provided most of the socio-cultural details, as well as a fairly extended portrait of Wajid both in his Lucknow and his Calcutta periods. [Luckily for Ray this wonderful book appeared in English just in time to be of use to him.]

3. The Indian histories of Mill and Beveridge, both critical of the Annexation.

4. Two histories of the Mutiny (by Ball and by Kaye).
5. *The Letters of Lord Dalhousie*. One of these letters provided the information that Outram grumbled about the new treaty and apprehended that Wajid would refuse to sign it. Dalhousie ascribes this attitude to indigestion [an idea that Ray has Outram specifically reject when talking to Dr Fayrer – see p. 44].
6. *The Reminiscences of Sir Alexander Fayrer*. Fayrer was the Resident Surgeon, Honorary Assistant Resident and Postmaster of Lucknow at the time of the takeover.
7. Two biographies of Outram (by Trotter and by Goldschmid).
8. The diaries and letters of Emily Eden, Fanny Eden, Bishop Heber and Fanny Parkes.
9. *The Indian Mutiny Diary* by Howard Russell. Russell came to India as the correspondent of *The Times*. He was on the spot when the British troops ransacked the Kaiserbagh Palace. He gives the only detailed description of the interior of the palace that I have come across.
10. The young Wajid's personal diary *Mahal Khana Shahi*. This turned out to be unending account of his amours. [Some think it spurious but Shama Zaidi does not.]
11. The text of Wajid Ali Shah's *Rahas* [the play he wrote about the god Krishna that is briefly performed by him at the beginning of the film].
12. Mrs Meer Hasan Ali's *On the Mussulmans of India* (1832). This was found useful for its details of life in the zenana.
13. *Umrao Jan Ada* (translated into English as *A Courtesan of Lucknow*). This gives a fascinating and authentic picture of Lucknow in Wajid's time.
14. All English and Bengali newspapers and journals of the period preserved in the National Library [at Calcutta].
15. I was also in close touch throughout with Professor Kaukabh of Aligarh University. Professor Kaukabh happens to be a great-grandson of Wajid Ali Shah and is considered to be one of the best authorities in India on Wajid.

In trying to assimilate this array of historical and cultural information along with Prem Chand's story to make a coherent whole with the potentiality of a screenplay, Ray faced certain formidable difficulties. First came the audience's widespread ignorance of the facts of the relationship between Britain and Oudh in the century leading up to the Annexation – in India as much as elsewhere: to which the film's ten-minute prologue seemed the only solution. Secondly, there was the fact that chess is not inherently dramatic on screen. Thirdly came the need to make the King sympathetic. Finally, an overall tone of voice had to be found that was in harmony with the pleasure-loving decadence of Lucknow, without seeming to condone it.

The third of these difficulties almost persuaded Ray to abandon the film. He felt a strong Outram-like aversion for Wajid Ali Shah, the more he discovered about his debauches. Both Saeed Jaffrey and Shama Zaidi at one time received letters from him declaring his doubts about whether he could portray the King successfully. When Zaidi wrote to Ray offering to translate Wajid's diary (in which he very explicitly describes his sex life from the age of eight) and his letters from Calcutta to his wife in Lucknow, Ray replied, 'Don't tell me all this because then I'll dislike him even more,' Shama recalls with amusement.

As Ray observes in his Preface to this collection, it was the King's musical talents that reconciled him to the rest of his character; a ruler who is capable of admonishing his tearful Prime Minister (whom he had first come to know at the house of a courtesan) with the remark, 'Nothing but poetry and music should bring tears to a man's eyes.' One is reminded perhaps of another Ray protagonist – the fossilized nobleman–aesthete in *The Music Room (Jalsaghar)*, who lives only for music. As Ray said: 'The fact that the King was a great patron of music was one redeeming feature about him. But that came after long months of study, of the nawabs, of Lucknow and everything.'

This became the key that unlocked the character of Outram too. Among the copious extracts from the sources Ray consulted that are carefully noted down in his bulky shooting notebooks on *The Chess Players*, one comes across this character sketch of Outram taken from Goldschmid's biography of him:

1. Refused to benefit from conquest of Sind [in which campaign Outram had been in command in 1843].
2. Hated pettifogging ceremony.
3. 'His manner natural and gracious; his speech is marked by

7

a slight hesitation when choosing a word, but it is singularly correct and forcible; and his smile is very genial and sympathetic.'

4. 'Quaint sense of humour', a good anecdotist.
5. 'He greatly appreciated music of a touching character. Sacred music always his preference.'

From this description, and knowing the universal dislike of Indian music by the British of the Raj, one can easily imagine Outram failing signally to comprehend Wajid Ali Shah's – 'our fat King's' – gifts as a composer, while seeing only too plainly his faults as a ruler. Indian 'impracticality' and Indian love of the inessential – as Outram sees it – baffle and irritate him as they have baffled and irritated the West from the beginning of its encounter with India. But Outram also finds Wajid Ali Shah intriguing. The scene in which he interrogates his Urdu-speaking ADC Captain Weston about the King's doings demonstrates Ray's insight into the nature of such cultural friction with exquisite skill, suggesting clearly (but never explicitly) the intimate links between nationalism, racialism and lack of imagination.

In Outram's utilitarian superior Lord Dalhousie, the Governor-General in Calcutta, the hauteur is palpable. The confident, mocking tone of his letters suggested to Ray not only the ironic tone of the film but also, quite directly, the sequence of cartoons in the prologue of the film explaining how the British steadily deprived the rulers of Lucknow of money, land and power while preserving their formal status. Dalhousie was responsible for the annexation of several Indian states before Oudh. In one of his letters – quoted in the film – he refers to Wajid Ali Shah sardonically as 'the wretch at Lucknow' and to Oudh as 'a cherry which will drop into our mouths one day'. Ray immediately decided to depict this literally in the film by showing a cartoon Englishman knocking the crowns off cherries and popping them into his mouth. Although the cartoons are brasher than one would like – one of the few slightly false notes in the film – they are an imaginative and amusing expression of the lack of imagination with which the East India Company generally treated the Indians it ruled: like pawns to be manipulated in a game of chess.

Ray counterpoints this lack with the very different failings of the two chess players, so wrapped up in their games that they barely understand the political game being played with their futures. It took him months of pondering to satisfy himself that such a counterpoint would work on the screen. The obstacle, as he put it to Jaffrey in a letter in May 1976, was

> to establish the idea of obsession – which is basic to the development of the story – with a game which is basically abstract and intellectual. If it had been *gambling*, there'd be no problem. But the beauty of the story lies in the parallel that Prem Chand draws between the game and the moves of the crafty Raj leading to the 'capture' of the King.

His solution calls to mind two of his earlier films about obsessions: *The Music Room* and *The Goddess (Devi)*. In each case he stresses the human element without ever losing sight of the object of obsession. Just as it is not essential when watching these films to be familiar with Indian classical singing or Kali worship (though it is a big advantage with *The Goddess*), one need have no knowledge of chess to appreciate *The Chess Players*.

However, Ray was no doubt greatly assisted by his former passion for the game in building on Prem Chand's basic conceit. Deftly, he finds a hundred ways on screen to express Meer's and Mirza's utter absorption in their private world, enriching his theme so naturally and imperceptibly that its final impact defies analysis. All his best films have been like this – *Pather Panchali, The Postmaster, Charulata, Days and Nights in the Forest, Distant Thunder*, to name some of them. He had grasped the importance of this way of constructing a film as far back as 1950 after watching *Bicycle Thieves* and a hundred other films in London, when he wrote to his friend Chandragupta in Calcutta (then assisting Eugene Lourié in Jean Renoir's *The River*), as follows:

> The entire conventional approach (as exemplified by even the best American and British films) is wrong. Because the conventional approach tells you that the best way to tell a story is to leave out all except those elements which are directly related to the story, while the master's work clearly indicates that if your theme is strong and simple, then you can include a hundred little apparently irrelevant details which, instead of obscuring the theme, only help to intensify it by contrast, and in addition create the illusion of actuality better.

9

Ray's theme in *The Chess Players* is strong and simple – that the non-involvement of India's ruling classes assisted a small number of British in their takeover of India – but the way he expresses it is oblique and complex. It is not at first apparent, for example, what Mirza's ignorance of his wife's dissatisfaction with him may have to do with Outram's intention to annex Oudh; but by the end the link is clear, when Mirza's cuckolded friend Meer remarks to him with comic pathos in their village hideaway, 'We can't even cope with our wives, so how can we cope with the Company's army?' This is the moment in the film where Ray intends the two interwoven stories to become one, the moment of truth where all the pieces in the puzzle fall magically into place. Rather than the shattering revelation of the ending of *Charulata* – where Bhupati suddenly perceives his complete failure to understand his wife – the ending of *The Chess Players* recalls Ashim's deflation by Aparna at the end of *Days and Nights*. Though painful, it is also funny, made bearable for Meer and Mirza by their continuing affection for each other.

Neither film has much story as such, but – to quote Naipaul again – 'terrific things happen' in the compass of few words. The entire Indo-Muslim culture of Lucknow is suggested in *The Chess Players*, rather as Renoir suggests French society between the wars in *La Règle du Jeu*. Music and dance figure prominently, as it is important for us to grasp their highly regarded position in Wajid Ali Shah's world. His decision finally to renounce his throne without a fight is communicated to his courtiers not through mere words but through a musical couplet, a *thumri* of the kind made famous by Wajid – in fact his most famous *thumri* in India today (of which Ray knew a variation as a boy in Calcutta):

> *Jab chhorh chaley Lakhnau nagari*
> *Kaho haal adam par kya guzeri . . .*

which may be roughly translated as:

> When we left Lucknow,
> See what befell us . . .

On the printed page in English it may lack impact, but when sung by Amjad Khan in a hesitant voice husky with emotion, it is moving.

In the later stages of making and releasing *The Chess Players* Ray must sometimes have felt the *thumri* could apply to him too:

> When I left Bengal,
> See what befell me . . .

After Herculean efforts to film the Company troops arriving in Lucknow – in the midsummer heat of Jaipur, since only there could the necessary elephants be made available – Ray managed to get the film finished by September 1977. But when it was shown to its prospective all-India distributors they withdrew their support, apparently dissatisfied with the classical nature of the film's songs and dances and its use of high-flown Urdu: they had obviously been anticipating more razzamatazz. 'Mr Ray has made the film for a foreign audience' was the comment Ray passed on to Jaffrey rather gloomily in a letter at the end of October. But he knew it had also received an excellent response at a screening in Bombay: so good, rumour has it, that it made some of the big guns in the Bombay industry conspire to prevent the film getting a proper release in India. The language of the film being Hindi/Urdu rather than Ray's usual Bengali, and the presence of Bombay stars (Amjad Khan and Sanjeev Kumar in particular), may have provoked industry fears of their own product being undermined.

Judging from the reactions to the film in the Indian press such fears were groundless: though the film had many admirers, most Indians misjudged it. They probably expected a more full-blooded treatment in the manner of Attenborough's (later) *Gandhi*; Ray's restraint and irony towards both sides did not please them. The hostile critic already mentioned (to whom Ray replied) complained that Ray gave no sense of the way that discontent over the Annexation helped to bring about the Mutiny. He wrote:

> Study the records of this period and you realise how glaring is Satyajit's failure in giving us a picture of a placid and uneventful Lucknow in which his characters move about like lifeless dummies in an empty shadowplay.

Abroad the film had a warm reception, though not by any means as warm as that for much of Ray's earlier work, including *Days and Nights in the Forest*. Probably the most perceptive comment came from Tim Radford in the *Guardian*: 'Satyajit Ray seems to be able to achieve more and more with less and less.' Most critics, however, found the film slow and many also found it mannered and, like most Indians, too bloodless for their taste. The *New York Times* was probably typical in saying that 'Ray's not outraged. Sometimes he's amused; most often he's meditative, and unless you respond to this mood, the movie is so overly polite that you may want to shout a rude word.'

Neither East nor West seemed quite satisfied with *The Chess Players*. Both wanted Ray to have painted his canvas in bolder colours. But, as he pointed out at the time,

> the condemnation *is* there, ultimately, but the process of arriving at it is different. I was portraying two negative forces, feudalism and colonialism. You had to condemn both Wajid and Dalhousie. This was the challenge. I wanted to make this condemnation interesting by bringing in certain plus points of both the sides. You have to read this film between the lines.

Most of Ray's films, as he has quietly but frankly observed on a number of occasions, can be fully appreciated only by someone with insight into both cultures. *The Chess Players* undoubtedly gains in meaning if one studies the history and forms of artistic expression of the Mughals and their successors, as well as the attitude to those successors epitomized by General Outram when he describes Wajid as 'a frivolous, effeminate, irresponsible, worthless king'. If V. S. Naipaul, himself one of the great writers of the century, is right in comparing Ray with Shakespeare, one may safely predict that people will still be watching *The Chess Players* and discovering new things in it for very many years to come.

A.R.

The *Chess Players* (*Shatranj Ke Khilari*) was first shown at the National Film Theatre as part of the London Film Festival on 3 December 1977. The cast included:

MIRZA SAJJAD ALI	Sanjeev Kumar
MEER ROSHAN ALI	Saeed Jaffrey
WAJID ALI SHAH	Amjad Khan
GENERAL OUTRAM	Richard Attenborough
KHURSHID	Shabana Azmi
NAFEESA	Farida Jalal
AULEA BEGUM, QUEEN MOTHER	Veena
ALI NAQI KHAN, PRIME MINISTER	Victor Banerjee
CAPTAIN WESTON	Tom Alter
DR JOSEPH FAYRER	Barry John

Producer	Suresh Jindal
Screenplay	Satyajit Ray, from a short story by Prem Chand
Lighting Cameraman	Soumendu Roy
Animation	Ram Mohan
Editor	Dulal Dutta
Art Director	Bansi Chandragupta
Wardrobe	Shama Zaidi
Musical score	Satyajit Ray
Dance Director	Birju Maharaj

MIRZA SAJJAD ALI, a *jagirdar* of Oudh
MEER ROSHAN ALI, a *jagirdar* of Oudh
WAJID ALI SHAH, King of Oudh
AULEA BEGUM, WAJID's mother
ALI NAQI KHAN, Prime Minister of Oudh
KHURSHID, wife of MIRZA SAJJAD ALI
NAFEESA, wife of MEER ROSHAN ALI
AQIL, NAFEESA's lover
HIRIA, KHURSHID's maid servant
MUNSHI NANDLAL, a Persian tutor
GENERAL OUTRAM, Resident of Lucknow
CAPT. WESTON, OUTRAM's ADC
DR JOSEPH FAYRER, Residency doctor
KALLOO, a boy

Locale: Lucknow, 1856

SCENE I

Close-up of a chessboard (cloth). A game is in progress. A hand enters from the right, hovers over the pieces, and moves a White Bishop. Another hand enters from the left, moves a Black Knight and captures a White Pawn. The game continues.

NARRATOR: Look at the hands of the mighty generals deploying their forces on the battlefield. We do not know if these hands have ever held real weapons. But this is not a real battle where blood is shed and the fate of empires is decided –

(Now we see the two players – MEER ROSHAN ALI and MIRZA SAJJAD ALI.)

Mirza Sajjad Ali and Meer Roshan Ali are only playing at warfare. Their armies are pieces of ivory, their battlefield is a piece of cloth.

(Titles.)

MIRZA: Check.

NARRATOR: Mirza Sajjad Ali has given check, which means Meer Roshan Ali must now protect his King.

(Close-up of MEER's White King.)

This is the White King, which is open to attack from the Red Minister.

(Close-up of MIRZA's Red Minister. Close-up of MEER ROSHAN ALI.)

Meer Sahib, save your King, for if the King is lost, the battle is lost.

(Close-up of MIRZA. He takes a pull at the hookah, finds it's gone out.)

MIRZA: Maqbool!

(Long shot. A servant runs up, takes the hookah and hurries out to replenish it. The camera stays on the two friends playing with great concentration.)

NARRATOR: Poor Maqbool! How often will he have to attend to these hookahs. For there will be many more battles fought on that piece of cloth today.

(The camera begins to move very slowly to MS of the two friends.)

It has been like this ever since the day the two friends

discovered this noble game. You may ask: have they no work to do? Of course not! Whoever heard of the landed gentry working? These are noblemen of the capital of Oudh: Lucknow.

(*Close-up of an arch in the Mughal style: the camera pulls back. Followed by domes and minarets.*)

After the passing of the Mughals in Delhi, Lucknow became India's bastion of Muslim culture.

(*A flock of pigeons in the sky. A group of noblemen watch from a roof-top while the pigeons perform their feats.*)

Not all their games had the elegance of pigeons . . . or kite-flying.

(*An open field with hundreds of men flying kites. Gaily coloured kites fight and cavort in the sky.*)

That notable culture had its cruel side too.

(*A cock-fight is in progress. It is brutal and the crowd is intensely excited by it.*

Close-up of throne: the camera pulls back. The throne is empty.)

This is the throne of King Wajid, who ruled over Oudh. But the King had other interests too.

(WAJID's Rahas, *with* WAJID *himself playing Krishna. He is surrounded by a bevy of pretty girls, playing* gopinis. *The accompanying music is a beautiful song composed by* WAJID:)

    Subha lagana subha sagana chhatra dharo mayee
    Sakala pandita mila lagana kundali banayee
    Nanda-nandanaki juga juga jeeyo
    Ayesey mohana rupa chanda sama jhalkayee.

(WAJID ALI SHAH, *surrounded by a crowd, plays the* tasha (*drum*) *at the great festival of Mohurrum.*

WAJID ALI SHAH *at night reclining among his harem, being gently fanned with whisks.*

Close-up of WAJID: *the camera pulls back to show* WAJID *sitting on throne.*)

Nevertheless, there were times when King Wajid sat on the throne.

(WAJID *sitting at a* durbar. *The camera moves in slowly to a close-up of the crown.*)

If he was not overfond of ruling, he was certainly proud of his crown. Only five years ago, in 1851, he had sent it to London to be displayed at the Great Exhibition.

(Contemporary views of the Crystal Palace Exhibition of 1851.*)*
But listen to what an Englishman in India had to say about
it.
*(Close-up of Lord Dalhousie's letter. An English voice reads it
out:)*
'The wretch at Lucknow who has sent his crown to the
Exhibition would have done his people and us a great service
if he had sent his head in it – and he would never have
missed it. That is a cherry which will drop into our mouths
one day.'
NARRATOR: The head of the Kingdom of Oudh to be eaten like
a cherry? Alas, words penned by the Governor-General of
India . . .
(Portrait of Dalhousie.)
But perhaps Lord Dalhousie was inordinately fond of cherries. How many he had eaten in the last ten years:
*(Animation showing crowned cherries with their crowns being
knocked off by Dalhousie and the cherry being swallowed in one
gulp.)*
Punjab, Burma, Nagpur, Satara, Jhansi. The only one left
is the cherry of Oudh, whose friendship with Britain goes
back a century to the reign of Nawab Shuja-ud-Daula.
*(Portraits of Shuja. Engraving of the Battle of Buxar, treaty
document and details showing clasped hands.)*
Nawab Shuja had been unwise enough to pit his forces
against the British: no wonder he was defeated. But the
British did not dethrone him. All they did was to make him
sign a treaty pledging eternal friendship and five million
rupees compensation. Ever since, the Nawabs of Oudh have
maintained this friendship.
*(Paintings of British fighting in Afghanistan, Nepal and
Burma.)*
When British campaigns needed money, the Nawabs opened
their coffers.
(Same detail of clasped hands as before.)
And whenever British wrath had been aroused by evidence
of Nawabi misrule –
*(Animation: the Nawab asleep on the throne, a cake with the
word 'Oudh' on it beside him. Governor-General struts in from
the right, looking daggers, taps sleeping Nawab on shoulder.*

17

Nawab wakes up with a start, hangs head in shame. Governor-General points peremptorily at 'Oudh'. Nawab takes out dagger, slices off a piece of 'Oudh', hands it to Governor-General. Governor-General gulps piece, lifts top-hat to Nawab and struts away.
Portrait of Ghaziuddin.)
Nawab Ghaziuddin's generosity so gratified the British that they gave him the title of King. It was Ghaziuddin who fashioned the crown . . .
(Move in to close-up of Ghaziuddin's crown. Cut to crown on WAJID'*s head (live).)*
. . . which Wajid Ali sent to London. Poor Wajid! If only you knew what was in the mind of the Resident of Lucknow whose name was General Outram.

SCENE 2

Interior Lucknow Residency. OUTRAM'*s study. Afternoon.*

The back of OUTRAM'*s head. He is smoking. There is a knock at the door.* CAPTAIN WESTON, *one of* OUTRAM'*s assistants, enters and hands* OUTRAM *a telegram.*
WESTON: From Cawnpore, sir. General Wheeler.
 (WESTON *hands* OUTRAM *the telegram and turns to go.* OUTRAM *calls him back.)*
OUTRAM: Weston –
WESTON: Sir.
OUTRAM: Have you ever seen a pigeon that has one black and one white wing?
WESTON: Ah, no sir.
OUTRAM: Well now – *(Reading from a document)* 'Jewan Khan, the keeper of the royal pigeons, received a *khilat*' – that's a reward, I suppose, eh?
WESTON: Yes sir.
OUTRAM: – 'of Rs. 2000 for producing a pigeon with one black and one white wing.' I find this a very revealing document, Weston. It's an hour-by-hour account of the King's activities dated the 24th of January. That's yesterday. Did you know that the King prayed five times a day?
WESTON: Five is the number prescribed by the Koran, sir.

OUTRAM: Surely all Muslims don't pray five times a day?

WESTON: Well, not all, sir, but some do.

OUTRAM: The King being one of them?

WESTON: The King is known to be a very devout man, sir.

OUTRAM: Is he? H'm . . . 'His Majesty listened to a new singer, Mushtari Bai, and afterwards amused himself by flying kites on the palace roof.' That's at 4 p.m. Then the King goes to sleep for an hour but he's up in time for the third prayer at 5 p.m. And then in the evening – now where is it? – 'His Majesty recited a new poem on the loves of the *bulbul*' –

WESTON: A bird, sir. The Persian nightingale.

OUTRAM: Ah-ha – at a *mushaira*. What's a *mushaira*?

WESTON: A *mushaira* is a gathering of poets. They recite the new poems.

OUTRAM: I see.

(OUTRAM *puts down the court diary.*)

Tell me, Weston, you know the language, you know the people here – I mean, what kind of poet is the King? Is he any good, or is it simply because he's the King they say he's good?

WESTON: I think he's rather good, sir.

OUTRAM: You do, eh?

WESTON: Yes sir.

OUTRAM: D'you know any of his stuff?

WESTON: I know some, sir.

OUTRAM: Well, can you recite it? Do you know it by heart?

WESTON: (*Taken aback*) Recite it, sir?

OUTRAM: Yes, I'm not a poetry man. Many soldiers are. But I'm curious to know what it sounds like. I rather like the sound of Hindustani.

(WESTON *remains silent, slightly ill-at-ease.*)

Are they long, these poems?

WESTON: Not the ones I know, sir.

OUTRAM: Well, go on man, out with it!

(WESTON *recites a four-line poem.*)

Is that all?

WESTON: That's all, sir.

OUTRAM: Well, it certainly has the virtue of brevity. What the hell does it mean, if anything?

WESTON: He's speaking about himself, sir.

OUTRAM: Well what's he saying? It's nothing obscene, I hope?

WESTON: No sir.

OUTRAM: Well, what's he saying?

WESTON: (*Coughing lightly*)

> Wound not my bleeding body.
> Throw flowers gently on my grave.
> Though mingled with the earth, I rose up to the skies.
> People mistook my rising dust for the heavens.

That's all, sir.

OUTRAM: H'm. Doesn't strike me as a great flight of fancy, I'm afraid.

(OUTRAM *rises from his chair slowly.*)

WESTON: It doesn't translate very well, sir.

OUTRAM: And what about his songs? He's something of a composer, I understand? Are they any good, these songs?

WESTON: They keep running in your head, sir. I find them quite attractive. Some of them.

OUTRAM: I see.

WESTON: He's really quite gifted, sir.

(OUTRAM *glances briefly at* WESTON *and begins to pace the room thoughtfully.*)

He's also fond of dancing, sir.

OUTRAM: Yes, so I understand. With bells on his feet, like nautch-girls. Also dresses up as a Hindu god, I am told.

WESTON: You're right, sir. He also composes his own operas.

OUTRAM: Doesn't leave him much time for his concubines, not to speak of the affairs of the state. Does he really have 400 concubines?

WESTON: I believe that's the count, sir.

OUTRAM: And twenty-nine 'muta' wives. What the hell are 'muta' wives?

WESTON: (*Fastidiously*) 'Muta' wives, sir? They're temporary wives.

OUTRAM: *Temporary* wives?

WESTON: Yes, sir. A 'muta' marriage can last for three days, or three months or three years. 'Muta' is an Arabic word.

OUTRAM: And it means temporary?

WESTON: No, sir.

(OUTRAM *raises his eyebrows.*)

OUTRAM: No?

WESTON: It means – er, enjoyment.

OUTRAM: Oh. Oh, yes, I see. Most instructive. And what kind of a king do you think all this makes him, Weston? All these various accomplishments?

WESTON: (*Smiling*) Rather a special kind, sir, I should think. (OUTRAM *stops pacing, stiffens, turns sharply to* WESTON.)

OUTRAM: *Special*? I would've used a much stronger word than that, Weston. I'd have said a *bad* king. A frivolous, effeminate, irresponsible, worthless king.

WESTON: He's not the first eccentric in the line –

OUTRAM: (*Interrupting*) Oh – I know he's not the first, but he certainly deserves to be the last. We've put up with this nonsense long enough. Eunuchs, fiddlers, nautch-girls and 'muta' wives and God knows what else. He can't rule, he has no wish to rule, and therefore he has no business to rule.

WESTON: There I would agree with you, sir.

OUTRAM: Good. I am glad to hear that. I have it in mind to recommend you for a higher position when we take over –

WESTON: Take over, sir?

OUTRAM: Take over, Weston. And any suspicion that you hold a brief for the King would ruin your chances. You remember that.

(Evening. The Muezzin's *call can be heard. On the banks of the Gomti some Muslim boatmen are praying. More Muslims are praying in an open field.* KING WAJID *prays in his private mosque.)*

*(*MIRZA SAJJAD ALI's *drawing-room.* MIRZA SAJJAD ALI *and* MEER ROSHAN ALI *are praying. The chesscloth is in its place with only a few pieces standing. A game had just been finished before prayer time.*
Prayer over, MIRZA *and* MEER *rise and prepare for another game. A servant brings a lamp.)*

MIRZA: Maqbool! Bring the hookahs.

MEER: Mirza Sahib, where did you find this piece of calligraphy?

MIRZA: You won't believe me. I found it in a junk shop, for fifty rupees. Do you like it?

MEER: It's very good.
(The two have started to arrange the pieces.)

MIRZA: No wonder: it's the work of Shamsuddin.

MEER: When you come to my house next, I'll show you an even better one. My wife likes it so much, she's hung it in the bedroom.
*(*MIRZA *is humming a* ghazal. *The pieces are arranged. It is* MEER's *turn to play.)*

MIRZA: Meer Sahib. I must remind you of an unbreakable rule of chess.

MEER: What rule?

MIRZA: If you touch a piece, you must move it.

MEER: But I always –

MIRZA: You don't. Last time you touched a Knight, hesitated, then moved a Pawn. And on another occasion . . .

MEER: I'm sorry, Mirza Sahib. I'll be more careful from now on.

MIRZA: Well, make your move.
(Carriage bells are heard outside. MEER *has just made his first move when a servant calls and announces that* MUNSHI NANDLAL SINGH *would like to see* MIRZA *Sahib.* MIRZA *is irritated by this interruption.)*
Show him in.
(They put on their caps. NANDLAL *comes in. Middle-aged, jolly, obviously a man of some standing and culture.* MIRZA *and*

MEER *greet him with a totally convincing display of warm welcome.*)

We haven't seen you for ages.

MEER: We were just talking about you.

NANDLAL: I hope I'm not disturbing you.

MIRZA: Not at all: we're honoured.

(NANDLAL *catches sight of the chesscloth.*)

NANDLAL: I see you're about to start a game.

MIRZA: Well, as a matter of fact –

NANDLAL: Then I'd better go.

MIRZA: No, no –

MEER: This is our fourth game of the day.

MIRZA: Do sit down, please.

NANDLAL: The game of kings, the king of games. I'm proud it was invented by an Indian.

MIRZA: I thought it came from Persia.

NANDLAL: No, it originated in India. Then it travelled to Europe.

(MIRZA *and* MEER *are intrigued.*)

I see you're playing the Indian way.

MEER: What other way?

NANDLAL: The British way.

MIRZA: Don't say the Company's taken over chess, too.

(*They all laugh.*)

NANDLAL: I learnt British chess from Mr Collins when I taught him Persian.

MIRZA: How does their game differ from ours?

NANDLAL: There's little difference. The piece we call the Minister is called the Queen in the British game. And the Queens are placed facing each other.

(NANDLAL *makes the necessary changes to demonstrate.*)

And the Pawn can move two squares in its first move. When a Pawn reaches the eighth rank it can be exchanged for a Queen.

(MIRZA *and* MEER *shake their heads.*)

MEER: I must say the British are clever.

MIRZA: But why change the rules?

NANDLAL: It's a faster game.

MIRZA: So they find our game too slow?

MEER: Like our transport: now we're to have railway trains, and the telegraph.

NANDLAL: The telegraph is here already – and I don't like it.

MEER: Why not?

NANDLAL: Bad news travels faster.

MEER: Bad news?

NANDLAL: Haven't you heard?

MEER: We hear nothing when we play.

NANDLAL: Meer Sahib, you can't laugh it off. I hear the East India Company plans to take over Oudh.

MEER: What!

NANDLAL: I came here to tell you.

(MIRZA *chuckles*.)

MIRZA: You may have learnt British chess, but you seem not to follow their moves. All these campaigns in Nepal, the Punjab, Afghanistan, where do you think the Company gets the money to fight them? From the King of Oudh, of course. How? It's very simple. Just tell the King he's ruling badly, and unless he pays up, the Company will take over. The King pays up. The Company hears the jingle of gold, and everything returns to normal once again.

NANDLAL: So you think the Company needs money again?

MEER: Of course. Do you think the railway and the telegraph cost nothing?

NANDLAL: You may be right. But I don't trust Lord Dalhousie. I hear that British troops have reached Cawnpore. What if war should break out?

MIRZA: Meer Sahib, just take down that sword, will you?
(MEER does not understand MIRZA at first. Then, nervously he gets up and lifts a large sword from a display on MIRZA's wall.)
Take it out of its scabbard!
(MEER obeys and shows the curved blade to NANDLAL.)
Do you know whose sword that was? You tell him, Meer Sahib.
(MEER is not very good at rhetoric, but has a go at it nevertheless.)

MEER: This sword belonged to Mirza's great-grandfather. Both our great-grandfathers were officers in King Burhan-ul-Mulk's army.

MIRZA: They were so formidable they struck terror into the enemy. In recognition of their valour, the King granted them estates . . . which we are living off to this day. So you see whose blood flows in our veins.
(MEER gives a nervous giggle.)

MEER: Whatever happens, the British can't stop us playing chess.

MIRZA: We're talking of war, and he thinks only of chess!
(NANDLAL laughs.)

NANDLAL: Don't worry, Meer Sahib. We may have invented the game, but it's the British who have taken it up.

MIRZA: And made the Pawn move two squares.
(They all laugh.)

NANDLAL: Well, I must take my leave.

MEER: So soon?

NANDLAL: I feel like an intruder. Mr Collins wouldn't answer the door to any callers when we played.

MIRZA: Then Mr Collins should not only have studied our languages . . . but our manners too.
(NANDLAL exits.)

NARRATOR: While the great-grandsons of Burhan-ul-Mulk's officers fought bloodlessly, another game was being played elsewhere.
(Close-up of LORD DALHOUSIE's hand signing a despatch.)

In Calcutta, Lord Dalhousie was preparing an important despatch.
(*Galloping despatch riders are seen against the sky.*)
It was sent by special courier. Calcutta is 600 miles from Lucknow. The horseman covered the distance in seven days.
(*The horsemen are seen against various landscapes.*)
In the evening of January 31, 1856, the despatch reached General Outram.
(*The riders against the skyline of Lucknow.*)

SCENE 3

MIRZA's *house. Night. The clock shows just after* 10.30.

KHURSHID, MIRZA's *wife, sits alone, in the* zenana. *A plangent song is heard in the background. In the drawing-room, another game is in progress. A full dinner is arranged on plates and dishes within easy reach of the players. It is clear that the meal has been going on for some time, and it is also clear that both are used to eating and playing at the same time.* MEER *has finished eating. Three servants come.* MEER *washes his hands and mouth in water poured into a basin from a jug, and then dries himself with a towel.*
MIRZA: Finished already?
MEER: You know I'm a small eater.

(*The zenana.* KHURSHID, MIRZA's *wife, stands at a door with a scowl on her face, watching the servants return to the kitchen.* RAHIM, *carrying plates and dishes, gives the dozing* MAQBOOL *a nudge.*)
RAHIM: The master wants you.
(MAQBOOL *wakes up with a start, springs up and trips. He runs off towards the drawing-room.* KHURSHID *calls out to her maid servant.*)
KHURSHID: Hiria!
(HIRIA *has been dozing too. She comes to with a start and lumbers to her feet.*)

(*Drawing-room.* MIRZA *puts a* paan *in his mouth and makes a move.* MEER *touches a Knight, then quickly withdraws his hand. There is an exchange of looks* – MIRZA's *being admonitory.*)

26

MEER: Sorry, Mirza Sahib. It'll never happen again. (*He moves a Bishop.*) Check.

(MIRZA *hadn't expected this move. It has put him in a tight corner. Just then* HIRIA *the maid servant comes and addresses her master from behind the door.*)

HIRIA: Begum Sahiba wishes to see you, sir.

(MIRZA *makes a face. He hates such summons from the zenana in the middle of a game. He deliberately keeps* HIRIA *waiting.*)

Begum Sahiba wishes to see you, sir.

MIRZA: What for?

HIRIA: She didn't say, sir.

(MIRZA *keeps looking at the game.* HIRIA *persists.*)

MIRZA: Tell her I'm coming.

(HIRIA *goes away.*)

(*Imitating his wife*) 'Did you enjoy the pulao, dear?'

MEER: Is that what she wants to know?

(*Zenana.* HIRIA *comes back to report.*)

HIRIA: Master says he is coming.

KHURSHID: When?

HIRIA: He didn't say.

(HIRIA *turns to go, yawning with great deliberation.* KHURSHID *calls her back.*)

KHURSHID: Hiria, tell him I have a headache: he must come at once.

HIRIA: Why didn't you tell me? I could have rubbed sandalwood paste on your brow.

KHURSHID: Just do as you're told.

(HIRIA *lumbers off.*)

(*Drawing-room.* MIRZA *now makes a move. A good, clever move.* MEER *is starting to ponder his response when* HIRIA *reappears.*)

HIRIA: Begum Sahiba has a headache. She wants to see you at once.

MEER: You'd better look in.

MIRZA: Say I'm coming.

(HIRIA *goes away, looking stern.*)

They don't say a word when you spend the night with a

whore . . . but when you stay at home and play a clean game, they pester you.

MEER: Why not go? It will take me some time to get out of this trap anyway.

MIRZA: Headache, my foot.

(MIRZA *gets up.*)

MEER: Tell her I thought the food was delicious.

MIRZA: Don't play around with the pieces.

MEER: You know I'd never do such a thing.

(Zenana, *Bedroom.* KHURSHID *is sitting on the* charpoy *with her back to the door.* MIRZA *comes in.*)

MIRZA: (*Oozing compassion*) Hiria says you have a headache . . .

KHURSHID: (*Laying it on thick*) As if you cared.

MIRZA: What do you mean?

KHURSHID: As if you had the least bit of sympathy.

MIRZA: But –

KHURSHID: Even if I were dying, you wouldn't give me a drop of water.

MIRZA: How can you say that? I left the game because you called.

KHURSHID: That stupid game.

(MIRZA *sits beside his wife.*)

MIRZA: Stupid game? Why, it's the king of games. It was invented in India and now the world plays it.

KHURSHID: Then the world is stupid.

MIRZA: Ever since I started to play chess . . . my power of thinking has grown a hundredfold.

KHURSHID: But you never think of me.

MIRZA: Of course I do: I came rushing as soon as Hiria told me.

KHURSHID: It was far better when you spent your nights with that singing woman. Now you sit hunched over that stupid bit of cloth and jiggle around those stupid ivory pieces. And I sit praying to God so you will finish early and come to bed. But the wretched game goes on and on and I go crazy sitting and waiting. I order Hiria to tell me stories to keep me awake . . . and she keeps repeating the same stories over and over and over again. And you sit there with your stupid game and your stupid friend –

MIRZA: Begum, don't run down my friend because you're angry with me.

28

KHURSHID: He sits there and doesn't know what game his wife is playing at home.

MIRZA: (*Getting angry*) Now don't gossip.

KHURSHID: Gossip? All Lucknow knows that his wife is carrying on with another man. Only you and your friend don't know.
(*The conversation has gone on far too long for* MIRZA. *He comes to the point.*)

MIRZA: Begum, if you have a headache –

KHURSHID: Who says I have?

MIRZA: What?

KHURSHID: I don't.

MIRZA: Then why did you send for me?
(KHURSHID *says nothing.*)
Well, I'll go then.
(KHURSHID *grabs hold of her husband who has just got up. There is a tussle which wakes up the dozing* HIRIA. *She overhears* KHURSHID.)

KHURSHID: Please don't go just yet.
(*With a knowing smile* HIRIA *dozes off again.*)

(*In the drawing-room* MEER *outlines possible moves to himself.*)

(*In the zenana* KHURSHID *has forced her husband to lie down with her above him.*)

MIRZA: What are you looking at?

KHURSHID: (*Cooing*) Your eyes.

MIRZA: My eyes?

KHURSHID: They're red from staring at those stupid pieces. I won't let you go back tonight.

MIRZA: But . . . Meer Sahib is waiting –
(KHURSHID *playfully gags his mouth.*)

KHURSHID: Please forget that game tonight.
(KHURSHID *is trying to work* MIRZA *up, using all her wiles, caressing him with all the tenderness she is capable of. She begins to unbutton his clothes.* MIRZA *mumbles from behind her gag.*)

MIRZA: What are you doing? It's so chilly.
(KHURSHID *pulls a coverlet over them both.*)

(*Drawing-room.* MEER *wonders about his friend. Why is he taking so long? He looks around then gets up. He tiptoes to the*

door, cocks his ears and tiptoes back. With a deft but casual movement, he shifts one of his Pawns to a more favourable adjacent square.)

(Bedroom. MIRZA *is lying on his back on the* charpoy, KHURSHID *above him. Both of them are silent.* KHURSHID *now releases him, her efforts having failed.* MIRZA *begins to button up his clothes. Horses pass in the night outside. A dog barks.* KHURSHID *sits on the edge of the bed, looking away.* MIRZA *stands up.)*

MIRZA: Don't be angry, darling. Don't be so glum.

(KHURSHID *says nothing.)*

The thing is –

KHURSHID: You don't love me.

MIRZA: I do love you, believe me. I'll prove it . . . tomorrow. My mind was elsewhere, with Meer waiting and the game half finished.

KHURSHID: You only care for that game.

(MIRZA *laughs with some embarrassment.)*

MIRZA: Tomorrow I'll finish early . . . and dine with you. I'll
show you how much I love you. All right?

KHURSHID: You love that game more than you love me.

(MIRZA *laughs again and gets up to go, humming a song to
cover his awkwardness.* MIRZA *exits.* KHURSHID *waits for some
seconds, breathing hard. Then –)*

KHURSHID*: Hiria!*

(HIRIA *appears.)*

Come and tell me a story: I want to stay awake all night.

(*Drawing-room.* MIRZA *comes in. He has assumed a studiedly
solemn air.* MEER *looks up. He is bright enough to notice the
ruffled hair and other tell-tale details such as a loose flap on*
MIRZA's *jama.)*

MEER: A bad headache?

MIRZA: Very bad.

MEER: Tch tch.

MIRZA: She was flailing her arms about. I feared she would have
a fit.

MEER: Tch tch. (*He sighs ostentatiously and then moves a piece.)*
Check.

SCENE 4

The Residency Union Jack flutters in the morning breeze.

NARRATOR: Next morning, General Outram had a meeting with
the Prime Minister of Oudh.

(OUTRAM *sits at his desk.* WESTON *is by his side to interpret.
The Prime Minister* ALI NAQI KHAN's *face registers the utmost
consternation.)*

ALI: (*In Urdu*) Resident Sahib, this will come to His Majesty as
a bolt from the blue. In his worst nightmares he could not
have dreamt of this from the Company Bahadur. I cannot
think what agonies he will suffer when he hears of this.

WESTON: (*Begins to translate.)*

OUTRAM: Just sum it up, Weston, will you.

WESTON: Sir, His Majesty will be shocked to hear this.

OUTRAM: Well, will you tell the Prime Minister that I'd like His

Majesty to go through the treaty and let me have his views as soon as possible. It's a matter of the utmost urgency.

WESTON: (*Translating* ALI's *reply*) The Prime Minister wishes to know, why the new treaty? What happened to the old one?

OUTRAM: Please tell the Prime Minister that despite repeated warnings from our Government His Majesty has made no efforts whatsoever during the last ten years to improve the administration here. And since this has caused considerable distress among the common people of the province our Government has no alternative but to take matters into their own hands.

WESTON: (*Translating* ALI's *reply*) The Prime Minister wishes to know how there can be talk of misrule when the people are so happy?

OUTRAM: Just ask the Prime Minister if he knows about Colonel Sleeman's report.

WESTON: (*Translates.*)

ALI: (*In Urdu*) Yes, I know about the report. Colonel Sleeman went on his inspection against His Majesty's wishes. Yet we bore the expenses for his tour, for all his eleven hundred people. Tents, elephants, provisions, everything . . . If he gave a bad report, that is our misfortune. If he had inspected the Company's Bengal –

(OUTRAM *interrupts impatiently.*)

OUTRAM: Mr Khan, there is no use wasting words. The Governor-General's decision is irrevocable.

(MIRZA's *house. Exterior. Afternoon.* MEER *walks up to the main door, and is immediately assailed by* MIRZA's *voice, raised in anger, coming from the direction of the drawing-room.*)

MIRZA: Ungrateful knaves! This house is burgled, yet none of you stirs out of bed. I'll have you all sent to prison. I treat you well and this is how you show your gratitude. Don't make excuses.

(*Drawing-room. All the servants in the household – five or six of them – are being ticked off en masse by* MIRZA. *The reason for this outburst is not clear from what we hear.* MEER *now enters and greets* MIRZA *who returns his greeting in a perfunctory*

32

way. He dismisses the servants with harsh words, and looks at
MEER *with a scowl.*)

MEER: Why all the excitement?

MIRZA: Some rascal made off with my chessmen.

MEER: What!

MIRZA: It's my fault: I should have kept them in the safe. They steal the clothes off your back these days.
(MEER *realizes the gravity of the situation.*)

MEER: What do we do now? I haven't a set of my own.
(MIRZA *paces about impatiently.*)
Why not let's go and buy a new set?

MIRZA: Meer Sahib, don't you know that shops are closed on Fridays?

MEER: And to think that I'd worked out such a beautiful new strategy . . . The entire day is ruined. However, as the poet says . . . (*He quotes some lines in Urdu.*)
(MIRZA *suddenly stops pacing. His eyes light up.*)

MIRZA: Meer Sahib, that old lawyer of ours . . .

MEER: Imtiaz Hussein Sahib?

MIRZA: Remember the south-east corner of his drawing-room?
(MEER *throws his mind back, then gives a beatific smile.*)

MEER: Indeed I do!
(*Imtiaz Hussein Sahib's drawing-room. In a corner of the drawing-room, on a table, is an elegant set of chessmen on a chessboard inlaid with ivory.* MIRZA *and* MEER *come into the room, accompanied by a* SERVANT.)

SERVANT: Please be seated, sirs. I shall inform the Vakil Sahib right away.
(*The* SERVANT *goes away.* MIRZA *and* MEER *slowly advance towards the table with the chessboard. Two chairs are placed invitingly on two sides of the table, though not facing it.* MEER *and* MIRZA *are left with no choice but to occupy them. They talk in whispers.*)

MIRZA: Considering all he's chiselled out of me in legal fees . . .

MEER: What about me, too?

MIRZA: He shouldn't refuse to lend it to us for a day.
(*A man in his early forties enters. This is* CHUTTAN MIA, *the Vakil's younger son.* MEER *and* MIRZA *rise and the usual greetings are exchanged.*)
Is Vakil Sahib in?

CHUTTAN MIA: Yes, he is. He's resting. He's in bed. Unconscious.

(MIRZA *and* MEER *exchange glances.*)

We've sent for the doctor. Please make yourself comfortable. He was all right in the morning. Allah willing, he'll recover soon.

MIRZA *and* MEER: Let us pray for his speedy recovery.

CHUTTAN MIA: If you will excuse me.

MEER *and* MIRZA: Certainly, certainly: don't let us detain you.

(CHUTTAN MIA *leaves. The two friends are alone again.* MEER *hums. Their eyes meet, then turn towards the chessboard. Silence reigns. The white pieces are on* MEER's *side, poised for battle. A tempting sight.* MEER's *fingers now approach a Pawn, slowly, tentatively. The fingers now touch the piece.*)

MEER: (Very softly) Sipahi, advance!

(MIRZA *replies by advancing a Knight.* MEER *is about to move his second piece when a* SERVANT *enters the room.* MIRZA *smartly withdraws his hand. The two friends are a picture of innocence. The* SERVANT *has brought sherbet on a tray. He puts it down on a table in the middle the room, walks over to the chess table, removes the chessboard and places it on the table in the middle of the room. In its place, to the consternation of* MIRZA *and* MEER, *he puts the sherbet. The* SERVANT *leaves.* MIRZA *taps his stick on the floor.* MEER *toys with the glass of sherbet. Then, with studied nonchalance, he gets up, walks over to the other table and moves a chess piece. He invites* MIRZA *to follow him.* MIRZA *gets up and is about to move a piece when* CHUTTAN MIA *returns.*)

CHUTTAN MIA: Father has regained consciousness. Come, he'll be happy to see you.

(MEER *and* MIRZA *hesitate, but are left with no choice.*)

(*Vakil Sahib's bedroom. Vakil Sahib lies covered in a blanket. Apart from his face, only his right hand is exposed, holding a string of beads. He looks close to death. There are others in the room, in various states of despondency. Prayers are in progress.* MEER *and* MIRZA *enter, led by* CHUTTAN MIA.)

MEER: Are you sure he's conscious?

CHUTTAN MIA: Yes, he was just talking to me. (*He bends over the prostrate figure and raises his voice.*) Father, Meer Sahib and Mirza Sahib have come to pay their respects.
(*In response, Vakil Sahib parts his lips, rolls his eyeballs, and tries desperately to speak. Clear symptoms of the nearness of death.* MEER *and* MIRZA *back away towards the door. As they are about to cross the threshold, loud wailing goes up inside the house.* MIRZA *and* MEER *stand listening for a few seconds, then make suitable gestures of respect towards the dead, and exit to freedom and fresh air.*)

SCENE 5

A room in one of the many palaces in the Kaiserbagh complex. Day.

A Kathak dancer, Bismillah Jan, is giving a recital for King WAJID, *who is surrounded by his usual cohorts. There are appreciative wah-wahs at suitable gestures and* WAJID *seems to have not a care in the world. The dance goes on for a couple of minutes when the Prime Minister,* ALI NAQI KHAN *enters. He takes his seat beside* WAJID. *When the dance finishes,* WAJID *dismisses the entire congregation, so that now only* WAJID *and* ALI *are left.* WAJID *gazes at his Prime Minister, waiting for him to speak.*
   ALI *bursts into tears.*
WAJID: Come now, that is enough.
   (ALI *can only shake his head and sob.*)
The Resident Sahib must have been singing ghazals to you. Nothing but poetry and music should bring tears to a man's eyes.
   (WAJID *becomes irritated.*
   ALI *at last controls himself. For the first time* ALI *looks* WAJID *straight in the eyes. He makes a great effort and says –*)
ALI: Your Majesty, you shall no longer wear the crown.

   (*An open space on the roadside where a ram fight is taking place. Day.*
   Close-up. A resounding crash as the heads of the two fighting rams collide. A large motley crowd surrounds the arena. Betting is going on, and there are shouts of 'Sohrab' and 'Rustum', the names of the two rams.)

BOOKIE: Double or quits?
  (*Behind the* BOOKIE *appear* MEER *and* MIRZA, *who crane their necks to get a glimpse of the fight.*)
  Bet on Sohrab! Bet on Rustum!
  (MEER *addresses the* BOOKIE.)
MEER: Tell me which is which?
  (*The* BOOKIE *points them out.*)
BOOKIE: Sohrab has the black face.
  (*The fight goes on, the excitement of the crowd rising to a pitch.* MEER *brings out some money and places his bet on Rustum.*)
MEER: One rupee on Rustum.
MIRZA: Why waste good money, Meer Sahib? Betting is not for us.
  (*It does appear for a moment that Rustum might win, and* MEER *gets involved in the general excitement.*)
MEER: Rustum! Rustum!
  (*But suddenly the tide turns in Sohrab's favour. Rustum averts a butt, sidestepping.* MEER's *face falls. The backers of Sohrab go wild with excitement.* MIRZA *pulls* MEER *away.*)

(*A park in Lucknow. Day. A drumbeat followed by a proclamation: 'By order of His Majesty the King of Oudh the*

36

public is warned that there will be severe punishment for anyone spreading rumours that the Company is taking over our realm. The Company forces are not marching on Lucknow. They are passing en route *to Nepal.'*

MIRZA *is sitting disconsolately on a park bench, eating nuts.* MEER *has been wandering near by. Everything is peaceful.* MEER *comes up.)*

MEER: Mirza Sahib –

MIRZA: Yes?

MEER: What is it that makes people spread rumours?

(MIRZA *doesn't answer. He is drawing an outline of a chessboard in the dust with the tip of his cane.)*

If anyone even mentions a takeover, I shall pull his tongue out.

(MIRZA *still makes no comment.)*

What a glorious day, yet we have to spend it in idleness.

MIRZA: Meer Sahib, for every problem there is a solution. One must know where to seek it. Let's go home.

(MIRZA's *house. Zenana. Late afternoon.* KHURSHID *sucks contentedly on her hookah.)*

(MIRZA's *drawing-room. The chesscloth is spread in the usual place.* MIRZA *and* MEER *are arranging pieces in the squares. They are very unorthodox pieces indeed. The Pawns are cashew nuts – eight with their skins and eight without; the Knights are limes, green and yellow; Bishops are tomatoes; Rooks are chillies; the Kings and Ministers are phials of attar, dark and light. The King-phials have their stoppers on, while the Ministers are without them.)*

MIRZA: Maqbool! Bring the hookahs.

MEER: I take my hat off to you, Mirza.

(MIRZA *rubs his hands. He obviously relishes his own inventiveness.)*

MIRZA: The Pawns are no problem. Neither are the King and the Minister. But you have to be very careful with the Bishops, the Knights and the Rooks.

MEER: Let me see . . . tomato is Bishop, lime is Knight, chilli is Rook.

MIRZA: Correct.

37

(*Zenana.* KHURSHID, *standing behind a screen, sees* MAQBOOL
preparing the hookahs.)

KHURSHID: Is the master back?

MAQBOOL: Yes, Begum Sahiba.

KHURSHID: Is he alone?

MAQBOOL: No, Begum Sahiba. Meer Sahib is with him.

KHURSHID: (*Suspicion growing*) They're not playing chess, are
they?

MAQBOOL: They are, Begum Sahiba: with nuts, spices and vegetables. Who knows what magic there is in that game?

(MAQBOOL *moves away with the hookah.* KHURSHID *realizes
her strategy has failed. For a moment it appears she might break
down. But she manages to pull herself together and exits.*)

(*Drawing-room.* MEER *moves a lime diagonally across the board
with a view to capturing one of* MIRZA'S *Bishops.* MIRZA *stops
him in mid-course with an amused reprimand.*)

MIRZA: Hold on, Meer Sahib. That's a *Knight.* Lime is Knight.
Tomato is Bishop.

(MAQBOOL *meanwhile brings the hookahs. At the door leading
to the zenana appears* KHURSHID. *She doesn't cross the thres-*

38

hold, but extends only her hands which hold the chessmen in a silver bowl. She flings the pieces towards the chess players, and departs. The pieces descend in a cascade over the two men and scatter all over the floor. Both MEER *and* MIRZA *are speechless for a few seconds.)*

MEER: Who fired that salvo?

(He calls out to MAQBOOL. *Sense has dawned on* MIRZA *at last. And he had thought it was the work of a thief!* MIRZA *turns grim. Meanwhile* MEER *and* MAQBOOL *pick up the pieces. Pawns and Knights and Rooks and Bishops are retrieved from unlikely places and placed in a heap on the chesscloth.* MIRZA *at last opens his mouth.)*

MIRZA: Meer Sahib, if you don't mind, from tomorrow we'll play in your house.

MEER: You know you are always welcome.

*(*MIRZA *now lifts the chesscloth by the corner and lets the improvised pieces roll out.)*

MIRZA: Maqbool, give these vegetables to the Begum Sahiba with my compliments.

SCENE 6

WAJID's *durbar room. Afternoon.*

The throne is empty. The camera pulls back from it and cuts to the KING *and the backs of his courtiers in a line. He is upbraiding them.*

WAJID: You have deceived me. All of you.

(The courtiers have no answer to this accusation. WAJID *starts pacing up and down in front of them.)*

I loved you more than my own kin. I put my trust in you. I gave you all powers. What have you done except line your own pockets? Nothing. Colonel Sleeman had warned me against you. I paid no heed to him. Now I know he was right. *(He now turns to* ALI.*)* And he was right about you too, Prime Minister.

*(*ALI *raises his eyebrows.)*

ALI: About me, Your Majesty?

WAJID: Yes, about you.

ALI: What sin have I committed, Sire?

*(*WAJID *now strides up to* ALI *and holds up* DALHOUSIE's *letter.)*

39

WAJID: You dare to ask me that? Why did you not throw this paper in the Resident's face? Should you not have asked what right the Company had to break the treaty? The Company may assume administration, but it has no right to depose the King. (*He now turns away from* ALI *towards the empty throne.*) It is all my fault. I should never have sat on the throne. (*He walks up to the throne, runs his fingers lovingly over the jewels that stud it.*) But I was young, and I loved the crown, the robe, the jewels . . . I loved the pomp and the glitter . . . (*He moves away from the throne.*) In the beginning I behaved like a true King. For a time, at least. Did I not, Prime Minister?

ALI: You did, Your Majesty. Of course you did.

(WAJID *walks over to the Dewan* BALKISHEN.)

WAJID: Remember my army, Dewan Sahib?

BALKISHEN: How can I forget, Your Majesty?

WAJID: The daily parades? And the names I gave my cavalry regiments? Banka, Tirchha, Ghunghru . . . And my army of women? Pretty girls in pretty uniforms on pretty horses? What a picture they made when they trotted by . . . (*For a moment he is carried away by the memories of this regiment, and almost acts out the jaunty movements of the girls on the horses. But the memory passes, and seriousness returns. He shakes his head.*) But the Resident Sahib would have none of it! Richmond Sahib it was. He said, 'Why bother with an army? Our British forces are guarding your borders. You yourself are paying for them. So why bother?' 'Very well, Richmond Sahib. Your word is law. I shall not bother.' But what will I do? I ask you. If a King stops bothering about his realm, what is left for him to do?

(*There is silence all around, heads bowed, everybody averting the King's eyes, everybody trying to hold down their sorrow.* WAJID *continues after a pause and a slight smile.*)

I found the answer. Resident Sahib never told me. No one told me. I found it myself. (*He turns to* ALI.) Do you remember that song of mine?

ALI: Which one, Your Majesty?

(WAJID *recites the first line of a* thumri.)

WAJID: Tarap tarap sagari raen gujari . . .
Kaun desa gayo, sanwariya!

ALI: I remember, Sire.

WAJID: Do you know when I composed it, and where?
(ALI *does not know the answer.* WAJID *points to the throne.*) It was here – on this very throne – in full court. (*Reminisces*) I shall never forget the moment. A man stood while his petition was read out.
(*Cut to a flashback.* WAJID *is on the throne in full regalia, the petitioner before him.*)

WAJID'S VOICE: Suddenly the clerk's voice seemed to fade away.
(*Here the camera slowly moves to a close-up of* WAJID. *His whole being expresses his emotion at the new composition. As the song continues we cut to the present. The courtiers murmur their appreciation.* WAJID *turns away.*)

WAJID: That was the answer I found. No, Prime Minister, I was never meant to rule. If my people had come to me and said, 'We do not want you, you are making us suffer', I would have cast away my crown then and there. But they did not say so. Do you know why? (*He turns round to face the courtiers again.*) Because I have never hidden my true self from them. I was not afraid to show how I was. And they loved me, in spite of that. (*With great fervour*) Even after ten years I can see the love in their eyes. They love my songs. They sing them. (WAJID *looks at* ALI.) Go and ask the Resident Sahib: how many Kings of England have written songs? Ask if Queen Victoria has composed songs which her people sing. (*He turns round and starts pacing again.*) The Company is sending troops. Why? Because the Company fears my people may rise against it. It knows my people are strong. Some of the Company's best soldiers are from Oudh. Is it not strange, Prime Minister . . . that my 'poor, oppressed people' . . . should make the best soldiers in the Company's army? (*He turns round slowly and walks back.*) Half of Oudh has already gone to you, Company. Now you want the other half and the throne too. You are breaking one more treaty in asking for it. If my people are badly ruled, why have they not fled to a realm you own? Why do they not cross the frontier and ask you to save them from my misrule?
(*He is silent for a few seconds. Then he walks up to the throne, ascends the steps and turns round. He addresses the* PRIME MINISTER.) Prime Minister, please go and tell the Honour-

41

able Resident my throne is not theirs for the asking. (*He sits down on the throne and grasps it in each hand.*) If they want it, they will have to fight for it.

(OUTRAM's *study. Late afternoon.* OUTRAM *is sitting smoking. Dr Joseph* FAYRER, *the young Residency doctor, is seated not far away. A bearer comes in with a lighted lamp and places it on the table.*)

OUTRAM: I don't like this damned business at all, Fayrer. Not one bit. And it certainly won't redound to the credit of John Company. You know my views on Sind?

FAYRER: I do, sir.

OUTRAM: We have even less justification for confiscation here than we had in Sind. Mind you, I meant every word I wrote in my report, and I fully endorse everything that Sleeman said. The administration here is execrable. And I don't like our fat King either. But a treaty is a treaty. I don't know whether you fully realize, but the King would be perfectly justified in insisting on the validity of the earlier treaty and refusing to sign the new one?

FAYRER: But wasn't the treaty of '37 abrogated by the Court of Directors?

OUTRAM: So it was, but by an inexcusable omission on the part of our Government, the King of Oudh was never informed.

FAYRER: Oh dear.

OUTRAM: Therefore – although we are fully entitled to take over the administration – we cannot dispense with the King, and we cannot appropriate the revenue. Nevertheless, I'm called upon to do my damnedest to get him to sign and abdicate, so that we don't lose face while we gain a kingdom. The King moves out, we move in – or rather, march in – Wheeler's troops are straining at the leash at Cawnpore – and we take over.

FAYRER: But what if he should refuse to abdicate?

OUTRAM: We still take over, Fayrer. The Annexation of Oudh is a *fait accompli.* (*He gets up, walks over to the window and looks out. The window overlooks the River Gumti and a part of Lucknow in the west.*)

To all intents and purposes, we're already standing on British territory, and our gracious Queen already has five million more subjects, and over a million pounds more in revenue. No, no – the question is not whether he will abdicate, but whether we can ensure a peaceful takeover. I'm afraid the answer is: no, we cannot. You know Oudh doesn't lack fighting men. Some of the pluckiest lads in our own troops are from here. Well, the King has his own troops, and so do a number of the feudal barons who stand to lose by our action. If these people rise in defence of the province, Wheeler will have no choice but to order his sepoys to fire on their own brothers. You see the dilemma?

FAYRER: I do indeed.

OUTRAM: I mean if – ha, *if* he decides to abdicate, he loses his throne, of course, but there are compensations. He gets a hundred thousand rupees a month as an allowance, and he's free to give up all pretence of having to rule. But who knows what he's going to do? Does anyone ever know? Does he know himself? He's certainly the biggest bundle of contradictions I've ever come across. I mean, a devout man who prays five times a day, never drinks and keeps a harem the size of a regiment! A king who sings, dances, versifies, plays the tom-tom, flies kites from the palace roof and struts around the stage surrounded by frolicking nautch-girls. My God, Fayrer, I've had dealings with Oriental monarchs before, but none to hold a candle to this laddie! I can't make him out. Can you?

FAYRER: Well, I know he can be obstinate. He's the only King in the entire Oudh dynasty who has refused to be treated by an English doctor.

OUTRAM: Who does he consult then?

FAYRER: Quacks, from what I can gather.

OUTRAM: Stubborn fool. I rather fear he's decided to be obstinate with us too. I sent him the draft treaty two days ago. I asked for a quick reply and none has yet come. Five days to go and still no word from the King. You know what that means? It means I shall have to ask for an interview. I get the wind up just to think of it.

FAYRER: I know you don't like them –

OUTRAM: Like them! The very thought unmans me, Fayrer. Can you think of anything more preposterous than the Royal embrace? And, upon my soul, Fayrer, what is that extra-ordinary perfume he uses?

(FAYRER *brings out his own handkerchief.*)

FAYRER: You mean this?

(OUTRAM *reacts strongly.*)

OUTRAM: My God, man, that's it.

FAYRER: It's attar, sir. Everyone uses it here.

OUTRAM: Attar?

FAYRER: An extract of rose. The damask rose, I think.

OUTRAM: Damask rose – d'you know that my uniform still reeks of it three months after my last interview. It would be a damned sight more convenient if he were in purdah too, like his womenfolk. At least one would be spared the extreme proximity.

FAYRER: Have you considered speaking to the Queen Mother?

OUTRAM: I have, I have. In fact I'm going to see her tomorrow morning. I'm told she's a very sensible woman.

FAYRER: Well, she's known to have given him good advice in the past.

OUTRAM: So I'm told. But I'm damned if I know what defines good advice in the present instance, Fayrer. Good for whom? Good for him? Good for us? Good for the Company? Good for the people? And why should she intercede on our behalf? Why shouldn't she take the King's side? After all, he is her own son, and we're throwing him out, are we not? . . . I don't like it, Fayrer. I don't like it at all, and yet I have to go through with it. That's the problem. And that's my complaint, Doctor, and there's nothing you can prescribe for it. Nothing.

SCENE 7

MEER's *house. Veranda in the zenana. Early afternoon.*

NAFEESA, *Meer's wife, hums and makes* paan. *She is about to put one in her mouth when she hears* MEER *shouting for his servant.*

MEER: Rafiq Mia!

(NAFEESA's *face darkens.*)

(Drawing-room. MEER *and* MIRZA. *Both are standing.* MIRZA *looks around admiringly.)*

MIRZA: Meer Sahib, this is an even better place than mine. So quiet: just right for chess.

*(*RAFIQ, *the servant, appears.)*

MEER: Bring the hookahs. And tell Begum Sahiba there are two for dinner.

MIRZA: You must show me the calligraphy your wife likes so much.

MEER: All in good time.

(Zenana. NAFEESA *is sitting behind a screen.* RAFIQ *speaks to her through it.)*

RAFIQ: The master's home, Begum Sahiba. Mirza Sahib is with him; he will dine with the master.

*(*NAFEESA *reacts strongly; there is barely concealed panic in her eyes.)*

NAFEESA: Very well.

(She gets up.)

(A lane near by. AQUIL, NAFEESA's *lover, is shown making his way through a narrow lane. He has to step aside to make way for a passing palanquin.)*

(Drawing-room. The pieces are arranged. The paan-*box is now opened preparatory to the game, and the two friends help themselves. The servants bring two hookahs.*

MEER: Have you made up with your wife? She seemed rather agitated yesterday.

*(*MIRZA *shakes his head.)*

What a problem!

MIRZA: *(Quoting a proverb)* Wives are always a problem.

*(*MEER *only chuckles.* MIRZA *gives him a glance.)*

Don't you agree?

*(*MEER *is anxious to start the game. He has White. He moves the first Pawn.)*

MEER: Some wives are a problem. No problem here, though.

(Lane. AQIL *enters* MEER's *house through the back door.)*

(Zenana. Veranda. AQIL *enters and is grabbed by an excited* NAFEESA.)

NAFEESA: Disaster! He's at home.

AQIL: What do you mean?

NAFEESA: He's in the drawing-room, playing chess. He's with his friend: he's never played here before. I'm so worried.

AQIL: So Uncle Meer's playing chess!

NAFEESA: Suppose something should happen?

AQIL: Don't worry: a man with his eyes on the chessboard is lost to the world.

NAFEESA: *(Hope rising)* That's just what he always says.

(Drawing-room.)

MEER: I don't wish to boast . . . but I'm the luckiest man in the

46

world. Look where you will, you won't find as sweet and reasonable a wife as mine. I haven't a single complaint to make.

(MIRZA *looks at him without saying a word.*)

(*Bedroom.* NAFEESA *and* AQIL *are on the bed.* AQIL *is demonstrating how well he can crack his fingers.* NAFEESA *is full of admiration for her lover's cleverness.*)

(*Drawing-room.*)

MEER: She even takes an interest in chess.

MIRZA: No! Really?

MEER: Yes. One day I explained the game to her and she appreciated its fascination. Now she even insists on my leaving early . . . so as not to keep you waiting.

MIRZA: Extraordinary!

MEER: And when I return home in the small hours, she rubs balm on my forehead and I am soon asleep.

MIRZA: (*Chokes*) That is luck indeed!

(MEER *suddenly remembers something and gets up.*)
Where are you going?

MEER: I'll fetch that calligraphy.

MIRZA: My respects to your wife.

MEER: Don't play about with those pieces while I'm away.

(MEER *laughs at his own joke, and goes out.* MIRZA *takes no notice of it.*)

(*Zenana. Bedroom.* AQIL *continues with his demonstration. Suddenly* MEER's *voice is heard, humming. The voice approaches. The lovers spring apart,* AQIL *rolling off the fourposter and landing on the floor. This is convenient, because he would in any case like to crawl out of sight under the bed. But before he can do so,* MEER *is in the room.* AQIL *is* MEER's *nephew, which explains why* MEER *is not shocked in the way one would expect him to be. He merely expresses extreme surprise, looking from his nephew to his wife and back. At this point,* NAFEESA *is more the resourceful of the two. She puts her finger to her lips.*)

NAFEESA: Sh-sh. (*She pushes* AQIL *down with her hand.*)
Don't come out. It's not safe yet.

MEER: (*Finding his voice at last*) What's going on?

NAFEESA: He's hiding.

MEER: That I can see. But why?

NAFEESA: They're after him.

MEER: Who? What have you done, Aqil? Was there a fight?

(MEER *spots* AQIL's *cane hanging over the door and feels even more disconcerted. But* NAFEESA *has run out of invention.* MEER *turns to* AQIL *on the floor.*) Say something! What happened?

AQIL: N–nothing.

(AQIL, *too, is desperately trying to make up a story that will fit the situation.*)

MEER: Who's after – ?

NAFEESA: Sh-sh.

MEER: (*Lowering voice*) Who's after him?

(AQIL *has found his story at last. He gets unsteadily to his feet.*)

AQIL: The army. The army is after me.

(AQIL *is up on his feet now.*)

MEER: But what army?

AQIL: Ours. The King's army.

NAFEESA: The King's army.

(AQIL's *story is now ready.*)

AQIL: They're rounding up people to fight the British, uncle.
Just grabbing them off the street.

(NAFEESA *enthusiastically agrees.*)

MEER: You know too?

NAFEESA: Aqil just told me.

AQIL: Officers came to our house.

NAFEESA: He sneaked out of the back door.

NAFEESA: Exactly.

MEER: I hope they didn't see you sneak out?

AQIL: I'm not sure, uncle.

NAFEESA: I heard them too. Just before you came. Clip-clop, clip-clop!

(MEER *is thoughtful. He turns to* AQIL.)

MEER: But . . . why hide under the bed? You can't be seen from the street.

AQIL: Er –

NAFEESA: He lost his head: he's like a child.

AQIL: I lost my head.

NAFEESA: Feel how his heart is racing.

(NAFEESA *takes* MEER's *hand and places it on* AQIL's *chest.* MEER *shakes his head. He is obviously worried for the boy.*)

MEER: (*To* NAFEESA) You'd better give him some hot milk.

(*He now turns to* AQIL.) Don't worry, my dear fellow: you're perfectly safe here.

(*Exit* MEER. AQIL *and* NAFEESA *sigh in relief and embrace each other.*)

(*Drawing-room.*)

MEER: They're calling at houses rounding up people to fight for the King.

MIRZA: Meer Sahib, you can be arrested for spreading such rumours.

MEER: Rumours? Aqil saw it with his own eyes.

MIRZA: Aqil?

MEER: He's my nephew, he's just told me what's going on.

MIRZA: When?

MEER: Just now. He was hiding under the bed. Poor boy, he's quite shaken: his heart is racing.

(MIRZA *has now sized up the situation.*)

The King's soldiers haven't been paid for months. They must have refused to fight. We must do something about it.

MIRZA: You mean you want to fight?

MEER: Me? What a notion!

(MIRZA *keeps looking at this gullible friend of his. He shakes his head and smiles.*)

MIRZA: Let's get back to our game.

MEER: How can I play when I know we're not safe here?

(MIRZA *loses patience.*)

MIRZA: Should we go back to my house?

MEER: Out of the question.

MIRZA: Well, we –

(*The sound of horse's hooves is heard.* MEER *turns pale.*)

MEER: (*Whispering*) It's them.

(MIRZA *gets up and goes to the window.*)

For God's sake, don't go out on the balcony! (*But* MIRZA *goes out to look. Two cavalrymen of Oudh are seen passing.*)

MIRZA: They don't seem to be looking for anybody. I tell you, there's nothing to worry about.

(MIRZA *sits down again but now* MEER *is on his feet. Behind him on the wall is a display of ferocious weaponry, similar to that in* MIRZA'*s house. The juxtaposition is so ridiculous that* MIRZA *begins to laugh.*)

MEER: Why are you looking at me like that?

(*But* MIRZA *is shaking with helpless laughter.*)

What are you laughing at?

MIRZA: I'm laughing at my friend . . . descendant of Burhan-ul-Mulk's brave cavalry officer.

(*He roars with laughter again.*)

MEER: (*Shaking him*) Pull yourself together and listen to me. We'll run away from here.

(MIRZA *dissolves into laughter again.*)

MIRZA: (*Pointing at the chessboard*) And leave that behind?

MEER: No, we take it. We'll play, but not here and not in your house either.

MIRZA: Where then?

MEER: In a village across the river there's a ruined old mosque. A quiet place, with not a soul around. The quietest, safest place imaginable.

MIRZA: You've seen the place?

MEER: With my own eyes. We'll leave at the crack of dawn and get back when it's dark.

(MIRZA *ponders the idea.*)

Nobody will recognize us. We'll take a mat and a couple of hookahs. We can buy our lunch from a shop – kebabs and chapatis.

MIRZA: What about weapons?

MEER: What?

MIRZA: We must carry weapons. A man who goes out unarmed in these troubled times never returns home.

MEER: All right, we'll carry pistols.

SCENE 8

The Queen Mother AULEA BEGUM's *chamber. Day.*

AULEA *is seated with her back to a Kashmiri shawl which is held up by two eunuchs to serve as a curtain. On the other side of the curtain are* OUTRAM *and his two ADCs:* WESTON *and* HAYES.
The interview has already started.

WESTON: Begum Sahiba, the Governor has seen the treaty.

OUTRAM: I have come to you, Begum Sahiba, because I know I can trust you to give your son good counsel, as you have done in the past.

WESTON: (*Translates.*)

AULEA: What if Begum Sahiba were to advise her son to order his troops to take up arms against the British forces?

WESTON: (*Translates.*)

OUTRAM: That, if I may say so, would be most imprudent.

WESTON: (*Translates.*)

OUTRAM: I have come here with only one purpose: to ensure that His Majesty signs the new treaty. And I would be greatly beholden to the Begum Sahiba if she would request His Majesty to do so.

AULEA: Resident Sahib, how can I ask someone to sign a treaty which I myself do not understand? Wajid Ali Shah was enthroned with the full consent of the Company Bahadur. If he proved to be a bad ruler, why did the Company not do something about it? Why did it not guide him to correct the administration? Why this sudden drastic step after ten years? Has my son ever defied the Company or made trouble for it? Resident Sahib, have you forgotten how you were received by our people when you first came here a year ago? Have you ever known such warmth and hospitality?

(WESTON *is about to translate, but* OUTRAM *stops him with an impatient gesture.*)

OUTRAM: Does the Begum Sahiba appreciate that His Majesty is being offered most generous compensation for the action that our Government is forced to take against him?

WESTON: (*Translates.*)

(*There is a perceptible pause before* AULEA *answers.*)

AULEA: Is not the Governor-General a servant of the Company?

WESTON: (*Translates.*)

OUTRAM: Yes, he is.

WESTON: (*Translates.*)

AULEA: Is he also not a servant of the Queen of England?

WESTON: (*Translates.*)

OUTRAM: Yes.

WESTON: (*Translates.*)

AULEA: Does the Queen of England realize how her servant is treating His Majesty who is servant of Almighty God and nobody else?

WESTON: (*Translates.*)

(OUTRAM *appears ill-at-ease.* AULEA *continues without waiting for an answer.*)

AULEA: Resident Sahib, tell the Governor-General that we do not want money. We want justice. If the Queen's servant cannot give us justice, we shall go to the Queen herself and ask for it.

(*The balcony of a room in the Kaiserbagh. Evening.*
WAJID *is sitting in the balcony, with his cat on his lap. There is a hushed group around* WAJID: ALI, BALKISHEN *and others, but* WAJID *seems oblivious of their presence.* ALI *reports an important event of the day in a muffled voice.*)

ALI: The Resident Sahib had an audience with the Queen Mother today. The Queen Mother has told him that she herself will go to England to seek justice from Queen Victoria.

(*There is no reaction from* WAJID *to all this. The Finance Minister,* BALKISHEN, *now speaks.*)

BALKISHEN: Our barons have also sent word. They await your

Majesty's order to raise an army of 100,000 men and 1,000 pieces of artillery to oppose the Company's forces.

(There is a pause. Through the window the sun is setting over the domes and minarets of Lucknow. At last, WAJID *opens his mouth. But he doesn't speak: he sings. Very softly, he sings the first line of a new song.)*

WAJID: Jab chhorh chaley Lakhnau nagari . . .

(The courtiers bow down their heads, touched.)

    Jab chhorh chaley Lakhnau nagari

    Kaho haal adam par kya guzeri . . .

(He repeats the first line and stops.) Company Bahadur! – You can take away my crown, but you cannot take away my dignity. *(He turns to his Minister.)* The Company has offered me a handsome allowance. As a citizen of Oudh, if not as its King, I must show my gratitude. Inform the Resident Sahib that I shall be pleased to receive him tomorrow at eight in the morning. But before he comes, dismount all guns and disarm all the soldiers, and instruct my people to offer no resistance when Lucknow is entered by the Company's troops.

SCENE 9

The Bara Imambara Gate. Dawn.

Shehnai *plays* raga Bhairon *in the* nahabatkhana. *Looking down a slope into the city with the Bara Imambara in the background.* MIRZA *and* MEER, *well wrapped up against the cold, carrying bundles, make their way up the slope towards a bridge. As they cross the bridge, the placid river is seen behind them. The King's soldiers throw down their weapons. The discarded muskets form a heap on the ground.*

The other side of the River Gumti.

MEER *and* MIRZA *are standing in the middle of a road, looking around. There are a few huts, but they seem to be uninhabited. To the south the Lucknow skyline can be seen shrouded in mist across the river.*

MIRZA: Well, Meer Sahib, where is your mosque?

MEER: I can see it clearly in my mind's eye. Even the tamarind tree right beside it.

53

MIRZA: Perhaps the British troops have razed it to the ground?

MEER: God forbid! God forbid!

(There is a boy of about thirteen, KALLOO, *standing a short distance away with a pellet-gun in his hand. He has been observing* MEER *and* MIRZA *with a great deal of curiosity.)*

Shall we ask that boy?

*(*MIRZA *calls him over.)*

MIRZA: There used to be a mosque here, a ruined mosque.

KALLOO: *(Shakes head)* There's one about two miles from here.

MIRZA: An old mosque?

KALLOO: No, built only the other day.

MIRZA: *(Turns to* MEER*)* Well, Meer Sahib?

*(*MEER *looks positively guilty now.)*

Perhaps you saw the mosque in a dream? Well?

MEER: I'm terribly sorry, Mirza Sahib. That mosque was in Cawnpore. I saw it as a child; one can't always be right, you know.

*(*MIRZA *glowers at his friend, speechless with anger.)*

As the couplet goes: 'I have spent all this time in awareness, and now . . .'

MIRZA: To hell with your couplet. Where do we play now? In that field of mustard?

KALLOO: You can come to my house, sir.

MIRZA: Who else is there?

KALLOO: Nobody – they've all run away.

MIRZA: Run away?

KALLOO: To Sitapur.

MIRZA: Why?

KALLOO: The British are coming, sir. What if they shoot people down?

MIRZA: Yet you've stayed?

KALLOO: I want to see them come, sir.

MIRZA: Aren't you afraid?

KALLOO: I like their red coats. They're coming today, sir, down that road over there.

MEER: What if war should break out? How do we get back?

MIRZA: Do you want to go back now?

MEER: Not at all.

MIRZA: Then you'll stay and play?

MEER: Certainly.

MIRZA: Definitely?

MEER: Definitely.

MIRZA: (*To the boy*) Very well, let's go to your house then. What's your name?

KALLOO: Kalloo, sir.

MIRZA: Achcha, Kalloo.

> (*Outside* KALLOO's *cottage.* KALLOO *comes out of the door carrying a* charpoy.)

MIRZA: Leave it, Kalloo. We have a mat with us.

> (MEER *and* MIRZA *have dropped their bundles on the ground and spread the mat. The chesscloth and the pieces, the hookahs, the* paan *boxes, everything is taken out of the bundles and put on the mat.*)

KALLOO: You're playing, sir?

MIRZA: Yes, chess.

MEER: Can you prepare a hookah, Kalloo?

KALLOO: Yes, sir.

MEER: Go on then: everything's here.

> (KALLOO's *eyes light up.*)

KALLOO: You'll give me baksheesh?

MEER *and* MIRZA: Of course.

MIRZA: Can you get us something to eat?

KALLOO: Now, sir?

MIRZA: No, when we're hungry.

KALLOO: I'll run to town and get anything you want.

MIRZA: Excellent.

> (KALLOO *notices the pistols, just coming out of the bundle. His eyes pop out.*)

KALLOO: Are you going to fight the British, sir?

MIRZA: Why not? We're not afraid of them. Are we?

> (MEER *gives a nervous laugh, stressing the fact that* MIRZA *is only joking.*)

> (*Palace interior in the Kaiserbagh. A clock on a mantelpiece shows half a minute to eight.* WAJID *is seated in a gilt chair, waiting for* OUTRAM. *Sound of marching boots is heard.* OUTRAM *and his two ADCs arrive at the door of the palace room and stop, clicking their heels.* WAJID *gets up and starts walking towards the door, followed by* ALI, BALKISHEN, *a*

young boy who is obviously WAJID's *son, and four other courtiers.*

OUTRAM *and the ADCs step over the threshold, walk across a few steps and stop. The two groups now stand facing each other.* OUTRAM *gives a stiff nod.* WAJID *walks over and embraces him. The group now walks across the room.*

WAJID *resumes his position on the gilt chair, while* OUTRAM *occupies the only other chair in the room, facing* WAJID. OUTRAM *beckons to* WESTON, *who steps over and stands behind him.*)

OUTRAM: We are most grateful to His Majesty for granting us this interview.

WESTON: (*Translates.*)

OUTRAM: We also appreciate his gesture in disarming his soldiers. We regard it, we hope rightly, as evidence of his concern to negotiate a peaceful conclusion to the treaty.

WESTON: (*Translates.*)

(WAJID *has been looking at* OUTRAM. *He now turns his eyes away from him.*)

OUTRAM: I would like if I may to make a personal request to His Majesty that he please sign this treaty and formalize his abdication.

WESTON: (*Translates.*)

(*Still no response from* WAJID.)

OUTRAM: I hope the King has understood what I've said.

WESTON: (*Translates.*)

(WAJID *now turns his gaze slowly in the direction of* OUTRAM *and keeps it fixed on him long enough to make* OUTRAM *feel uncomfortable. Now* WAJID *turns his gaze towards* WESTON. WESTON *is unable to meet it, and drops his gaze.* WAJID *rises from his chair and slowly approaches* OUTRAM. OUTRAM *has also risen. Standing before* OUTRAM, WAJID *takes off his turban and offers it to him.* OUTRAM *is bewildered.*)

OUTRAM: What is this?

(WAJID *keeps his hand stretched out with the turban held lightly between his fingers.*)

Would you please tell His Majesty that I have no use for that.

WESTON: (*Translates.*)

WAJID: (*With great feeling*) I can bare my head for you, Resident Sahib, but I cannot sign that treaty.

SCENE 10

KALLOO's *house. Courtyard. Early afternoon.*

MIRZA *and* MEER *are playing. There are hardly a dozen pieces left on the board. There are more Black casualties than White.* MEER *has White.* MIRZA *touches a piece then withdraws. He exchanges glances with* MEER. *He then makes a move.*

MEER: You're sure? (*He indicates what he will do next.*) You can take it back.

MIRZA: It's all right.

(*He slaps a mosquito which has landed on his neck.*)

MEER: As you wish.

(MEER *captures* MIRZA's *Minister.* MIRZA *swats another mosquito. We can see his irritation growing.*)

I'm afraid you'll lose this time.

MIRZA: No wonder. These mosquitoes are draining my blood.

MEER: They don't seem to bite me.

MIRZA: They're choosy: they only go for pure blood.

57

(MEER *gives a short laugh.*)

MEER: Check.

(MIRZA, *his eyes on the board, takes at pull at the hookah. It's gone out. His temper rises.*)

MIRZA: Where the hell is that boy? Kalloo!

MEER: You sent him to fetch the food.

(*On a sudden impulse,* MIRZA *takes the hookah and gets up. He'll have a go at preparing it himself.*)

Can you manage that yourself?

(MIRZA *looks around in the house but can't find the tobacco. He emerges again.*)

MIRZA: It's well past noon and still no sign of food.

MEER: How helpless we are without servants. As the verse goes . . . (*He quotes it.*)

MIRZA: You're in high spirits today.

MEER: I feel wonderful. The General is about to win the battle: my strategy has paid off.

(MIRZA *makes a move.* MEER *crows with pleasure.*)

What an ideal spot this is. No officers to harass us . . . and the British can come and go for all we care.

MIRZA: (*With eyes on board*) You must have slept well, thanks to the balm your wife rubs on your brow.

MEER: (*Still sensing no threat*) That's true of every night.

(MIRZA *still has his eyes on the pieces, but one can see irritation getting the better of discretion.*)

MIRZA: I wonder where Aqil places himself while your wife does her massage?

(MEER *stiffens.* MIRZA *looks up at him and then back to the board.*)

Under the bed, I suppose.

MEER: What do you imply?

(MIRZA *glances up.*)

MIRZA: Your move.

(MEER'*s look is a mixture of pain, disbelief and admonition.*)

MEER: It's a dirty trick to put me off my game, just because you're losing.

MIRZA: Who's losing? I've moved; now it's your turn.

MEER: You've beaten me so often, and I've never lost my temper.

MIRZA: Your move, Meer Sahib.

MEER: One doesn't expect it from a gentleman.

(MIRZA *throws discretion to the winds.*)

MIRZA: Does a gentleman let his wife carry on with any man that comes her way?

(*This is too much for* MEER. *He brings all the venom he can into his words.*)

MEER: You've no right to talk like that. You forget that your ancestors were nothing but grass-cutters.

(MIRZA *suddenly grabs hold of* MEER's *shawl.*)

MIRZA: And what about your ancestors, slaving away in the kitchens of –

(*But* MIRZA *freezes in mid-speech.* MEER *has picked up a pistol and is pointing it straight at him.* MIRZA *is forced to let go of* MEER. *He draws back, reaches for the other pistol, but* MEER *kicks it out of his reach.* MEER *now rises to his feet, steps back, gun aimed at* MIRZA. MIRZA, *too, rises, shaken, incredulous, panicky.* MIRZA *suddenly feels desperate.*)

Have you lost your senses? You must be insane. Throw away that stupid gun.

MEER: When I'm really angry, I can kill.

MIRZA: All right, kill me. Pull the trigger then. But what I've told you is the truth.

MEER: A lie!

MIRZA: I swear it's true. I can vouch for it.

MEER: I don't believe you.

MIRZA: You'll find out for yourself one day: then you'll regret it.

(*By now* MIRZA *has almost got used to the gun. Perhaps at heart he doesn't believe that his friend can use it on him.*)

MEER: You're saying this to upset me, so I lose the game.

MIRZA: That's a vile thing to say, Meer Sahib. Do you think I could ever be so mean? It's you who cheated in the past, but I never said a word.

(*Suddenly we hear* KALLOO's *voice, screaming.*)

KALLOO: (*Off-screen*) The British are coming! The British are coming!

(MEER, *startled by the unexpected shout, accidentally presses the trigger, and the pistol goes off.* MIRZA *grips his arm.* MEER *looks stunned.*

In the distance is the army, marching up, the red coats blazing in the afternoon sun. A long column of animals, men and guns, flying a Union Jack. KALLOO *watches spellbound.*

MEER *is looking with deep apprehension at* MIRZA. MIRZA *slowly removes his hand from the shawl which covers his arm. There is no blood on the shawl, but a small portion of the delicate embroidery has been holed and frayed by a brush from the bullet.* MIRZA *is relieved, but unnerved by the narrowness of his escape.* MEER *subsides with relief.*

The troops pass in front of the camera filling the air with a great sound of clattering hooves, marching feet and rolling artillery.

MEER *now realizes that there is no need for commiseration, since* MIRZA *is unhurt. He walks away. The wall between the two remains.*

MIRZA *is seated on the* charpoy, *profoundly shaken.* MEER *is disappearing in the distance.*

The sound of the marching troops dies away.

KALLOO *appears, panting. He addresses* MIRZA.)

KALLOO: The food, sir.

(MIRZA *doesn't reply.*)

The food, sir.

(*Still no reply.*)

There was such a crowd in the market. Everybody shouting and running one way and another. That's why it took me so long, sir.

MIRZA: Put it on the mat.

(KALLOO *walks over, puts the package down on the mat, and brings out some money from his pocket.*)

KALLOO: Here's the change, sir.

MIRZA: Keep it.

KALLOO: Our King has given up, sir. The British have become our rulers.

(MIRZA *reacts, looking at* KALLOO *for the first time.*)

There was no fighting, sir. No guns went off.

(*As the* NARRATOR's *voice takes over, the camera shows a series of skylines of Lucknow in the pale light of dusk.*)

NARRATOR: You're right, Kalloo. No fighting, no bloodshed. Wajid Ali Shah has made sure of that. Three days from today, on February 5th 1856, the Kingdom of Oudh will be in British hands, Wajid Ali Shah will leave his beloved city, for all time, and Lord Dalhousie will have eaten his cherry.

(Now we are back with MEER *and* MIRZA. *The sound of* azaan *comes floating over the Gumti from the mosque.* MIRZA *is now seated on the mat, eating a belated lunch. He sees* MEER *approaching.)*

MIRZA: *(Affectionately)* Meer Sahib, the food is getting cold.

*(*MEER *advances with heavy steps. As he comes nearer, we notice a white smear on his shawl. Bird-dropping.* MIRZA *notices it.)*

I see you've been standing under a tree?

*(*MEER *looks gloomy. He still doesn't bring himself to look at* MIRZA.*)*

MEER: Even the crows despise me. The British take over Oudh, while we hide in a village and fight over petty things.

MIRZA: We couldn't have done much even if we'd stayed in town.

MEER: If we can't cope with our wives, how can we cope with the British army?

MIRZA: Yes, you're right. So why worry?

MEER: I'm not worrying about that.

MIRZA: What are you worrying about, Meer Sahib?

*(*MEER *looks at* MIRZA *for the first time: a brief, timid, tentative glance.* MEER *suddenly looks very lonely, very vulnerable.)*

MEER: About who to play chess with.

*(*MIRZA *is truly touched. He looks at* MEER *with warm sympathy.)*

MIRZA: Here is one person, Meer Sahib. And there is some food; we can eat and play at the same time. When it's dark, we can go home. We need darkness to hide our faces.

*(*MEER *nods, recognizing the truth of this.)*

Come, let's have a fast game.

*(*MEER *walks over to where* MIRZA *is sitting.)*

MEER: A fast game?

*(*MEER *slowly sits down.)*

MIRZA: Yes, a fast game. Fast, like a railway train.

*(*MIRZA *picks up the Minister.)*

Move over, Minister. Make way for Queen Victoria!

(The camera freezes on a close-up of the Queen in MIRZA's *hand. This dissolves into a view of the two friends playing their first game of British chess in the wan light of a late winter afternoon, as the sound of* azaan *mixes with that of a bugle, sounding the retreat.)*

A GAME OF CHESS

by Prem Chand
Translated by Saeed Jaffrey

It was the age of Nawab Wajid Ali Shah, and his capital, Lucknow, was steeped in subtle shades of decadence and bliss. Affluent and poor, young and old, everyone was in the mood to celebrate and enjoy themselves. Some held delightful parties, while others sought ecstasy in the opium pipe. All of life was charged with a kind of inebriated madness. Politics, poetry and literature, craft and industry, trade and exchange, all were tinged with an unabashed self-indulgence. State officials drank wine. Poets were lost in the carnal world of kisses and embraces. Artisans experimented with lace and embroidery designs. Swordsmen used their energies in partridge and quail fights, while ordinary people indulged in the new fashion for rouge and mascara, and bought fresh concoctions of perfume and pomade. In fact, the whole kingdom was shackled to sensuality, and in everyone's eyes there was the glow of intoxication caused by the goblet and the wine flask. About the rest of the world, the advances and inventions which knowledge and learning were making, how western powers were capturing areas of land and sea, no one had the slightest idea. They cared only for the quail fights and the bets being laid while partridges parried and thrust in the ring. *Chausar*, a kind of Monopoly, was played with great zest – people endlessly discussed manoeuvres and counter-manoeuvres, and great games of chess. Whole armies were lost and won – but only on the chessboard!

The Nawab was in even worse condition. In his quarters, new musical techniques and melodies were being devised, new recipes and forms of enjoyment were carefully pondered. If you gave alms to a beggar, he would not buy bread with it but would spend it on opium or hashish. The heirs of the rich sharpened their tongues with repartee, and gained other kinds of wisdom in the houses of pleasure.

The game of chess was considered ideal for self-advancement, for the maturing of wisdom and sharpening of the intellect. Even today there are descendants of those people who advocate it enthusiastically.

62

So if Mirza Sajjad Ali and Meer Roshan Ali spent most of their lives in 'sharpening their intellect' in this way, no one could point an accusatory finger at them. Whatever else the uninitiated might have thought of them, these two were gentlemen of leisure and owned inherited property. How else could they spend their time but by playing chess? Soon after sunrise, having breakfasted, they would open their chessboard and arrange the pieces with elaborate ceremony. And then the process of sharpening the intellect would begin. They were so engrossed in the game that it didn't matter when noon came, or the afternoon, or when dusk descended. A servant would come and announce that lunch or dinner was ready, and was always told, 'Set the places, we'll come.' But compared to chess, the best *korma* curry and the finest of *pulaos* seemed insipid. In desperation the poor cook would often just leave the food in the drawing-room, and then the two friends would satisfy two appetites simultaneously, proving their dexterity at both eating and playing chess; but sometimes the food would remain untouched.

There were no elderly relatives living with Mirza Sajjad Ali, so most of the chess bouts took place in the drawing-room of his house. This did not mean that the members of his household were happy with his pastime; on the contrary the household servants, and even other servants from the locality, from maids to housekeepers, gossiped enviously: 'What a wretched terribly unlucky game; it's ruined many a home. God forbid that anyone should acquire a craving for it – he will be able to serve neither God nor man! He will become like the proverbial dhobi's dog, welcome neither at home nor at the riverbank. It's an incurable malady!' Even the lady of the house, the Begum, raised her voice every so often in protest against this pastime. But the opportunities to do so were rare, as she would still be asleep in the mornings when her husband stole away towards the chessboard, and he would return at night long after she had fallen asleep again. She would vent her anger on the wrong people, mainly the hapless servants who were at hand. 'So, he wants *paan*, does he? Ask him to come and fetch them himself. It's not as though his feet are smeared with henna paste and he can't walk!' Then: 'What did you say? He has no time to eat? Go and smash the plate over his head! I don't care if he feeds the dogs with it or eats it himself – we can't wait for him any longer!' But the irony of it was that the Begum found her husband less at fault than his partner, Meer Sahib. She referred to Meer Sahib scathingly as a fool, an evil influence and a sponger. It is quite possible, too, that Mirza, defending his own absence, put the entire blame on Meer.

One day the Begum had a headache, so she said to her maid, 'Go and fetch Mirza, and ask him to get a doctor. Go on now, run. My head is going to explode!' When the maid conveyed this message to Mirza, he merely said, 'You go back, I'm on my way.' The Begum was furious. She could not stand the idea of having a headache while her husband played chess regardless. 'Go and tell him that if he doesn't come, I'll go to the doctor myself – I don't need him to show me the way!' By now Mirza was in the middle of a most interesting game; in just two moves he could beat Meer Sahib. 'It's not as though she was dying,' he couldn't help saying. 'Can't she wait? The doctor's not some magician who will abracadabra the headache away!' Meer Sahib replied, however, 'I say, do go and listen to her – women have a very delicate temperament.' Mirza answered sarcastically, 'Yes, why don't I go now? Only two more moves and I've finished!' 'I too have thought of a move to *stun* you into defeat,' said Meer, 'but please go and listen to her. Why break her heart over such a small thing?'

Mirza grumbled, 'But I feel like defeating you *now*.'

Meer replied, 'I refuse to play now – please, go and speak to her.'

'But my dear fellow,' answered Mirza, I'll have to go all the way to the doctor's for nothing; she hasn't got a headache – it's just an excuse to annoy me.'

'Whatever it is, you can't just ignore her.'

'Oh, all right, then – just let me make one more move.'

Meer was firm: 'Absolutely not. I shan't touch a piece until you've been to see her.'

When Mirza Sahib finally entered the Begum's chamber, she complained bitterly. 'You love that wretched chess so much, you don't even care if someone's dying. You just can't tear yourself away from it. It's not chess at all – it's your mistress and my rival! You really behave dreadfully to me!'

'But what could I do?' Mirza replied. 'Meer Sahib simply

wouldn't let me leave; it's only with great difficulty that I've managed to extricate myself from his clutches.'

'Does he think everyone is as big a fool as he is?' said the Begum. 'He's got a wife and children too – or has he got rid of them?' Mirza stayed calm. 'The fellow's a complete addict. Whenever he comes and bullies me, I am forced, out of sheer politeness, to play with him.' But the Begum snapped back: 'Then why don't you shoo him away, like you would a dog?'

'Praise Allah!' said Mirza. 'He's my equal! In age and rank even more than an equal. I can't just dismiss him!'

'So let *me* shoo him away!' the Begum retorted. 'If he gets angry, let him. We're not dependent on him!'

As they say, if the Queen sulks, she merely shortens her own happiness. Nevertheless, the Begum called out for her maid. 'Go and fetch the chessboard, and tell Meer Sahib that my husband will not play now. Please tell him to leave and never to show his face here again.'

Mirza stepped in. 'Please – don't do such a terrible thing! Do you want to drag me down? Wait, Abbasi, where are you running to, you wretched woman?' The Begum called the maid back.

'Why don't you let her go? Anyone who stops her drinks my blood! All right, you've stopped her, have you? Let's see how you stop *me* now!'

Having said this, the Begum stormed out towards the drawing-room. Mirza's face was ashen. He commanded his wife, 'For God's sake, I swear on the Martyr of Karbala, Imam Hussain, that if you step out, you will see my own corpse leave this house!'

The Begum was adamant, and kept on moving, but suddenly at the door to the drawing-room the thought of being seen without a veil in front of a strange man stopped her. She leaned through the doorway, only to find (by a happy accident) the room completely empty! Meer Sahib had changed one or two pieces to suit him, and, as though to protest his innocence, had left the room and was walking nonchalantly on the veranda outside.

This was an opportunity not to be missed. The Begum's prayers had been answered. She marched into the room and began to disrupt the chess game totally, hurling some pieces under the divan and flinging others outside before bolting the door from the inside. Meer Sahib, who was close to the door, saw the chess pieces being flung out and from the feverish jingle of bangles deduced that the Begum was furious. Quietly he went home.

Mirza scolded the Begum, saying that she'd done a terrible thing. The Begum merely replied, 'If that fool ever sets foot here again, I'll turn him out immediately! He thinks this is a whore-house, not our home! If you'd shown as much devotion to God as to chess, you two would've become prophets by now! Is it fair that you should keep playing chess, while I fret over what goes into the oven and the spice-grinder! Am I a slave? Please go to the doctor this minute! What are you waiting for?'

When Mirza left the house, mortified, instead of going to the doctor he went to Meer's house and, in deeply apologetic tones, told the whole story.

Meer Sahib laughed and said, 'I realized as much when the maid brought the message about the headache. I knew that the omens weren't good today. But she does seem extremely hot-tempered. Phew! What a cheek! You've pampered her too much. It's not right! What business of hers is it what you do outside? It's her duty to look after the household. It doesn't become her to interfere in men's affairs. Just look at my house; no one dares say boo!'

'Well, anyway, just tell me where we play now,' Mirza interrupted.

'Don't worry; I've a large enough house – we shall play here,' replied Meer cheerfully.

'But how can I calm down my Begum?' Mirza said. 'When I stayed at home to play she was angry enough, but if I leave the house, she'll kill me.'

'Oh, let her rant and rave, dear fellow – in two or three days she'll come round; but be a little stiff with her, too.'

For whatever reason, Meer Sahib's Begum actually preferred him to be absent from the house. She had never complained about his pastime. Indeed, if he was late in getting away, or felt lazy, she would lecture him on the virtues of punctuality and urge him to go. For this reason, Meer Sahib had come to think of his wife as having the most amiable disposition, and was convinced that she was the personification of female virtue. But now, when her own drawing-room had become the chess rendez-vous, and Meer's constant presence began to interfere with her freedom, she became irritable. 'How can I get rid of this curse?' she asked herself.

The situation was becoming rather difficult for the servants of the house too. They began to whisper and grumble among themselves. Until now, they had been able to slouch around and snore all day, not caring who came to and from the house. Their sole duty was going to the bazaar twice a day; that was all. But now they were on duty night and day. Sometimes they were ordered to fetch *paan*, at other times, water; sometimes ice would be demanded and sometimes a refill of tobacco. As for the hookah pipe, it was constantly kept smouldering away, like a broken-hearted lover! All of them would go to the Begum and moan: 'His lordship's addiction to chess has become a nightmare. We run errands all day; what kind of a game *is* this which takes from dawn until dusk to finish! Why can't they play for just an hour or two, and that's it – the end? And also, as your ladyship knows, it is bad luck to play it; whoever becomes addicted can't survive. In one form or another disaster befalls his house. Whole districts have been ruined. People point at us, making us die of shame.'

'I can't stand the sight of the game, either,' the Begum would reply; 'but what can I do? What power do I have?'

There were a few wise old men in the district who also started to predict disaster. 'There is no escape now. When our nobility has become so effete, only God can save the country! This kingdom will be ruined by chess! The omens are bad indeed.'

In fact, the whole realm of Oudh seemed to be in trouble. People were being burgled daily, and there was no one to listen to their complaints. It was as though the entire wealth of the villages was sucked into Lucknow, where it was spent on providing all manner of articles of pleasure. Jesters and mimics, *Kathak* dancers and providers of bliss held sway.

Gold pieces rained down on the shops where drink or opium were sold; the sons of the rich would throw a sovereign for a single puff. While this lavish spending was going on, the debt to the English Company kept increasing day by day. No one cared a jot how it was to be repaid. Even the yearly revenue could not be paid. The Representative of the Company kept on writing letters of warning and even made threats. But the people here were driven by the intoxication of self-indulgence, and no one gave a damn.

Many months passed with the games of chess being played in the drawing-room of Meer Sahib. New moves were constantly invented, new strategies devised and destroyed. Sometimes they would quarrel while playing and even become abusive; but these small grievances would soon disappear. Sometimes Mirza would go home in a huff and Meer Sahib would pick up the chessboard, go inside, and swear never to go anywhere near a game of chess again. But by daybreak the two friends would be together again, sleep having evaporated all the unpleasantness of the previous day.

One day, while the two gentlemen were sitting there, diving in and out of the labyrinth of chess, an armed cavalryman from the Royal Regiment arrived, asking for Meer Sahib. Meer was terrified. 'God knows who the devil this is,' he said. He ordered all the doors of his house shut and told the servants to say he wasn't in.

'If he's not at home, where can he be? He must be hiding somewhere!' the cavalryman responded.

The servant said, 'I don't know about that. This is the reply I've got from the house. What is your business?'

'How can I tell you what my mission is!' retorted the cavalryman; 'He has been summoned by His Majesty. Perhaps they need more men for the army. Is he a landlord, or some sort of fraud?' The servant replied, 'Please take your leave; we shall inform his lordship.'

'It's not a matter of informing,' the cavalryman said; 'I shall come back early tomorrow, search the house and take him with me. My orders are to present him myself.'

With that, the cavalryman left, and Meer Sahib felt as though his own soul had gone too. Trembling with fear, he went to Mirza, saying, 'What can we do now?'

Mirza only answered, 'What a terrible calamity! Perhaps they will summon me too!'

'But the wretched fellow has threatened to come again tomorrow!' Meer insisted.

'If this isn't the wrath of heaven, then what is?' cried Mirza.

'If they really want to enlist more soldiers, then we're as good as dead! The mere mention of battle gives me the shivers.'

'Even now I've lost my appetite for food and drink,' mourned Meer.

'The only way out is not to confront him at all,' proposed Mirza.

'Let's just disappear – then let the whole city come and look for us, they won't find us. We'll play chess in some wilderness across the River Gomti; our friend will come here for us, and leave empty handed!'

Meer was thrilled, 'Bravo! What a brilliant idea! By God, from tomorrow morning, across the Gomti it shall be!'

Meanwhile, the Begum Sahiba was busy laughing with the cavalryman. 'You disguised yourself superbly,' she said. He laughed, 'I can snap my fingers at those idiots and they'll dance! My husband's brain and guts have been devoured by chess! See if he spends any time at home after this. Once he leaves in the morning, he won't dare to come back till late at night!'

From that day on, the two friends would leave the house in the darkness before sunrise, a small folded carpet under their arm and a packet of *paan* in their hand. They would go across the River Gomti and set up camp in an old ruined mosque, which was probably left over from the age of the Mughals. On their way, they would pick up a *chillum* holder, some tobacco and pieces of coal. On reaching the mosque, they would lay down the carpet and the chessboard, fill the *chillum*, light it, and start to play. Then they would be completely oblivious to all matters of this world and the next. 'Move, check, checkmate': apart from these cries, no other words passed their lips. Their absorption in the game was more intense than that of the most self-hypnotized mendicant. In the afternoons, whenever they felt hungry, the two gentlemen would walk through the narrower lanes of the town, find a working-men's café, and eat there. After a smoke of their *chillum* they would once again sink into their game of chess. So deeply, in fact, that on the odd occasion they didn't even bother about eating.

But meanwhile, the labyrinths of the political chess game being played in the country were becoming more and more elaborate. The forces of 'John Company' were steadily advancing towards Lucknow. There was panic in the city, people gathering up their wives and children and fleeing to the countryside. Such disturbances were of no concern to our two chess-playing friends, however. On leaving the house, they would seek out the narrower lanes to avoid being seen, and the local people seldom saw their faces.

By now the English forces had almost reached Lucknow.

One day when the two gentlemen were engrossed in their game – Meer Sahib was losing and Mirza Sahib was outmanoeuvring him with every move – suddenly, what should they see but the English Army marching along the road right in front of them! The Company had decided to invade Lucknow; it wanted to devour the whole kingdom as a form of repayment of its debt. It was the age-old ruse of the money-lender; the same old trick that has enfeebled so many nations that, today, they find themselves in shackles.

Meer Sahib said, 'The English forces are coming.'

'Let them come,' said Mirza. 'Save your hand. Check.'

'But we must have a look,' Meer answered. 'Let's take cover and peep. What powerfully built youths they are! It terrifies me just to look at them.'

'You can see them later,' said Mirza. 'What's the hurry? Yet again, check.'

But Meer was excited. 'The artillery is here too. There must be about five thousand men – scarlet faces like red monkeys.'

'My dear sir, don't make excuses. Here. Check,' Mirza said.

'You really are an incredible man,' replied Meer. 'Please think about this – if the city's occupied, how are we going to get home?'

'When it's time to go home we'll think about it – here, check and checkmate.'

The army moved on. The two friends started a fresh game. Mirza asked, 'What about eating today?'

'I'm fasting today – why, are you hungry?' asked Meer.

'Not really,' replied Mirza. 'Who knows what might be happening in the city?'

'Nothing might be happening in the city,' snapped Meer impatiently. 'People will be resting after dinner. His Majesty, the Life of the World, will also be resting – or perhaps he's enjoying a round of drinks.'

This time, when the friends sat down to play, they continued until three o'clock. Then they heard the sound of the army coming back. Nawab Wajid Ali Shah had been dethroned. He was under arrest, and the army was taking him away. There had been no trouble in the city at all – no warrior had shed a single drop of blood! The Nawab took leave of his kingdom in exactly the kind of weeping way that a young bride leaves home for her in-laws' house. The Begums, his wives, wept also. The maids and the housekeeper wept: a great kingdom had come to an end. From the beginning of time no king had ever been dethroned in such a peaceful and non-violent fashion, or at least history has recorded no such example. But this was not that *ahimsa*, that non-violence which pleases the gods. It was gutless impotence which made them weep. The ruler of Lucknow was made to march as an ordinary prisoner, while his own city of Lucknow slept on unconcerned in the sleep of decadent bliss! This indeed was the nadir of political decay.

Mirza looked up from his game. 'Those brutes have imprisoned our noble King!' 'Really?' responded Meer. 'Are you a judge suddenly? Here, check.'

But Mirza was anxious. 'Pause a while, dear sir. I'm in no mood to concentrate on the game just now. Our highest lord the Nawab must be shedding tears of blood. This day, the Light of Lucknow has gone.'

'Yes, of course he'll be crying,' said Meer. 'He won't get the luxuries he's used to in a foreign prison, I assure you. Check.'

'No one's life continues unchanged for ever. These really are hard times, a curse of the Heavens,' replied Mirza thoughtfully.

'Indeed, indeed,' replied Meer, vaguely, 'again, check. It'll be checkmate next; you can't escape, you know.'

'Oh my God, how unfeeling you are!' cried Mirza. 'You are witness to such a terrible event and yet you feel no sorrow? After the departure of our king, Light of the World, there's no connoisseur of the arts left! Lucknow has become desolate!'

'Please save the life of your *own* King first!' Meer replied; 'Then mourn the demise of "our Glorious Lord". Here. Check and checkmate. How about that?'

The English Army was taking the Nawab away in front of their very eyes, but as soon as it had disappeared over the horizon, Mirza set up a new game. 'The sense of hurt that accompanies defeat is terrible,' said Meer Sahib. 'Come, let us write an elegy on the miserable plight of the Nawab.' However,

Mirza's sense of loyalty and feeling for poetry had vanished with his defeat at chess and he was itching to take his revenge.

It was evening. In the ruins of the mosque the bats seemed to be calling the faithful to prayer. Swallows settled in their nests and prayed the *Maghrib* prayer of dusk. Our two players, on the other hand, were still embroiled in their game, like two bloodthirsty warriors fighting for their lives. Mirza had lost three consecutive games, and nor did the fate of the fourth one look at all promising. Over and over again he was willing himself to win, playing with great caution, keeping perfect control on his wits, but sometimes he was making such a bad move that he ruined the entire game for himself. Meer Sahib, on the other hand, was in high spirits, reciting *ghazal* poems, singing *thumri* melodies and snapping his fingers in glee. He would cry out, calling upon not only the district, but the world, to recognize his genius. He was as pleased with himself as if he'd unearthed some buried treasure. Mirza Sahib found this good humour extremely irritating. Raising an eyebrow, he would reproach his friend: 'Please don't change your moves. What are you doing? You make a move and then immediately change it! Whatever you have to do, think hard before doing it. And, sir, why do you always keep your finger on the piece? Please leave the pieces alone. Until you're convinced in your heart what move to make, don't even touch the piece! And why are you taking half an hour to make a move? This is most irregular. From now on, whoever takes more than five minutes over a single move will be considered to have lost the game. Look! You altered your move again! Please put that piece back where it was.'

Meer Sahib's Bishop was vulnerable, so he said: 'When did I move?'

Mirza was getting cross. 'You've already moved! You're advised to put the piece back where it was!'

Meer said, 'Why should I put it back? When did I even *touch* the piece?'

'You may talk of not touching it, but it's still considered a move,' snapped Mirza. 'You saw that your Bishop was vulnerable, so now you're trying to cause confusion.'

'You're the one who causes confusion,' Meer retorted. 'Victory and defeat are in the hands of fate. No one can succeed just by causing confusion.'

72

'But you've lost this game.'

'How have *I* lost the game?'

'Put the piece back where you first had it.'

'Why should I put it there? I will not.'

'You'll have to.'

'I certainly will not.'

'Even your guardian angel would say put the piece back!' shouted the exasperated Mirza. 'Just who do you think you are?'

The argument got worse. Both defended their positions and neither would concede a point. The argument became a real quarrel, as other, more personal criticisms, intended to embarrass and humiliate, were dragged in.

'How can you be expected to be familiar with the rules and laws of chess, when all your ancestors did was cut grass!' sneered Mirza. 'Aristocracy is something else altogether; you don't become an aristocrat merely by being left some property!'

'Your own dear father must have been a grass-cutter then,' said Meer. '*Our* family has been playing chess for generations.'

'Rubbish!' shouted Mirza. 'Your people spent a lifetime slaving as cooks to the Nawab Ghaziuddin, and as a reward for that you were granted some property. And today you call yourselves aristocrats! Being a true aristocrat is not a game!'

'Why are you ruining the reputation of your own ancestors?' Meer retorted. '*They* might have been cooks. *Our* elders sat at the same table as the Nawab, eating the same food as him and sharing his goblet.'

'Some people are entirely shameless!'

'Hold your tongue or you'll regret it! I'm not used to forgiving such insults! If someone so much as casts the slightest aspersion at my family, he gets his brains scrambled!'

Mirza was calmer: 'Kindly desist. You have no idea of my family's courage. Come, let us test our fates, and see where we are to go.'

'Yes, certainly. Who's afraid of you!' Meer declared coolly.

The two friends drew swords from their waists. In those days rich and poor alike carried at their waist a poniard or dagger, a sword or a large knife. Though our two heroes were indolent men, they were not without honour. National valour was at its lowest ebb with them, but personal pride they possessed in plentiful quantity. While any passion for politics had died within them – 'Why should we die for the King or his kingdom or for the country?' they felt. 'Why disturb our sweet sleep of apathy?' – when it came to personal matters they showed absolutely no fear. If anything, they'd show complete ruthlessness.

Being familiar with bamboo fights and the judo-like *gatka*, they moved into position. Swords flashed. Sounds of combat filled the air; both were wounded and, writhing in agony, they both gave up the ghost there and then. Men whose eyes would not shed a tear for their King, cut their own throats over a chess Bishop!

It was dark now. The chessboard was spread out. Both Kings were seated gloriously on their royal thrones, but there seemed sadness in their faces, as though they were mourning the death of our heroes.

Silence reigned all around. The falling walls of the ruin, its crumbling arches and dust-laden minarets peered down at the corpses and grieved at the frailty of human life compared to any stone or brick.

DELIVERANCE

DELIVERANCE (SADGATI)

Satyajit Ray has frequently been accused of lacking anger and 'commitment' in his work, especially in comparison with his Bengali contemporary Mrinal Sen. One would have thought that an unprejudiced viewing of *Deliverance*, the fifty-minute film he made for Indian television in 1981, might have scotched that criticism for good; but it seemed to have almost the opposite effect, at least on Ray's critics in India, if not on the general Indian audience.

'Your film has caused not resentment but dissatisfaction,' wrote one angry critic, sparked off by a statement from Ray that he would continue to stand up to government censorship, even if other film-makers could not. 'Your whole objective [in *Deliverance*] is to bring about the death of [the Untouchable] Dukhi as fast as you can. So you resort to one-line or two-line sequences. Since you do not know the poor, you contrive them into desired situations. *Except the Brahmin, no one else emerges as a credible human being* [my italics]. Having made such a film you seek to don the mantle of the social revolutionary that you are not, either by intent or by inclination. You are a portrait artist. That is what your total output suggests.'

A different critic found the film far *too* challenging. 'At the risk of being shouted down by the realism lovers (all rich and comfy folks) one would suggest that morality themes should replace the stark cold-bloodedness of *Deliverance*. In matters of caste India is still not ready for the bitter truth *per se*. It must be sugar-coated for easy consumption with the dosage increasing gradually or the reaction could be negative . . . When the Brahmin in *Deliverance* carefully, oh so carefully, loops a rope around the dead Harijan (Untouchable) and lifts his leg in the crook of a twig to avoid touching him, the truth of it is too much. I wouldn't do that, says the viewer, I am a better man than you. Instant switch-off.'

My own view of *Deliverance*, taking it together with all Ray's films (and perhaps especially his first one, *Pather Panchali*), is that it proves that Ray is one of the most committed directors in the history of the cinema. Committed, that is, to human beings and to the primacy of their moral sense – rather than to money, power, property, institutions, political parties, religion or any other ideology. It is because Ray feels injustices in Indian society so keenly that he cannot make films about them that are glib, rhetorical or emotionally gratifying. The ending of Lindsay Anderson's *If*, for instance, 'which is a kind of poetic explosion, was something that Satyajit almost didn't see the necessity for. That's very revealing,' Lindsay Anderson has remarked of his old friend. More tellingly perhaps, Ray refused to yield to Government pressure to make a film in the 1975–7 Emergency, unlike many other film-makers: 'I reminded them I was a very bad propagandist,' he says today.

His decision to make *Deliverance* was prompted at least partly by his experience with the Government about five years later. He had applied for permission to make a documentary about child labour, the thousands and thousands of girls and boys forced out to work long before their proper time. His idea was to show simply shots of children at work without commentary. Permission was refused – on the grounds that child labour does not officially exist in India.

This diktat annoyed Ray. He started looking for a story 'which had strong cinematic elements which could be told as a gripping narrative, and which would also serve a function as a portrayal of really poor people'. These requirements all came simultaneously, he has said; one was not more important than another. 'Had "Sadgati" been less gripping or less cinematic, I wouldn't have considered it, although it might have been telling about the poor people.'

The milieu of the Prem Chand story he chose – a village in a rural district near Benares – is typical of the 300 or so short stories and fourteen novels that 'the father of contemporary Hindi fiction' wrote before his death in 1936. Prem Chand's particular perspective was one of sympathy for the oppressed in the small towns and villages; in this respect 'A Game of Chess' is an anomaly in his work.

Although 'Sadgati' was published in 1931 Ray found it necessary to change remarkably little in it to create a film about the contemporary situation. This in itself speaks volumes for the power of orthodoxy in the villages and the grip of the local élites – whether Brahmins or otherwise – over the lower classes. The most significant alteration Ray made was to set the film in a village near Raipur in Madhya Pradesh (central India), rather than near Benares – a change that was more than justified by the fact that the Untouchables of that area had migrated from the same area as that of Prem Chand's story, fleeing upper-caste tyranny: only to fall under its yoke once more in Raipur.

Ray's own state of West Bengal, because of its historic prosperity and its confluence of religions – Buddhism, Islam, Christianity and many reformist movements within Hinduism – has not experienced widespread caste-consciousness in its most rigid, merciless form, unlike, say, the neighbouring states of Bihar or Madhya Pradesh. Ray's own family has been notably free of caste as far back as his grandfather, although two of his grandfather's brothers were relatively orthodox Hindus. His grandfather and father – both distinguished men artistically speaking – were Brahmos, members of a movement of reformed Hinduism founded around 1830 that attracted some of the most creative, vigorous Bengalis of the colonial period. Satyajit himself ceased Brahmo worship in his late teens and says firmly, 'I'm not conscious of belonging to any caste at all at any time.'

Few of his countrymen would be as categoric as that about caste. Its existence is often cited as the reason why India is said to have preserved its identity despite the endless invasions of the subcontinent. While Ray accepts that caste may have had a rationale in 'the early stages of Indian history' – after the Aryan invasions – he says that

> there's no question that eventually, in time, it proved very wrong, and certainly created barriers which were very unpleasant. So I have nothing to defend in caste at all – nothing at all. Or in orthodoxy. I'm firmly against that kind of orthodoxy which is based purely on religion because I don't consider religion to be that important. I mean, what can you say in favour of orthodoxy which creates this division between people? And puts up a wall which is so artificial?

Despite his critics' belief to the contrary, Ray's constant preoccupation as a film-maker and as a man has been the breaking down of barriers to human contact. If he does not use a sledgehammer to achieve this in *Deliverance*, it is because he is fully aware of how entrenched the barriers are and that progress lies in trying to influence those who raised the barriers, rather than in launching a fruitless assault on the barriers themselves. Throughout his life and work he has felt that anger controlled is much more efficacious than anger displayed. 'I feel *Deliverance* is a deeply angry film,' he said in 1982, 'but it is not the anger of an exploding bomb but of a bow stretched taut and quivering.'

The film's shocking impact derives from its elemental theme combined with its acute, ruthless observation of people. Dukhi, the *Chamar* (a tanner and therefore of a very low caste), and Ghasiram, the Brahmin priest whom he forlornly approaches to arrange the correct ritual preparation for the marriage of his young daughter, are both very convincing individuals; but as the film progresses they become symbols too – in a manner unusual in Ray's films – of the oppressed locked in a centuries-old lethal embrace with the oppressor. Ghasiram is exceptional for Ray in being untouched by conscience, virtually indifferent to the man who begs his assistance in the name of religion and eventually perishes in his service. 'I think this is what happens when you have 2,000 years of orthodoxy,' Ray has said. 'You think you're doing the right thing. You think this is what is expected of you. You think that this will lead you to heaven, and not pollute you. So you have justification for everything you do – spiritual justification.'

This incisive judgement on the vast majority of what passes for religion and spirituality in India is the very marrow of *Deliverance*. Although the ending of the film, in which Ghasiram – desperate to dispose of Dukhi's corpse – drags it through the fields like a carcass to its final resting place among animal skulls, is the film's harshest scene, an earlier scene is perhaps even more devastating. Ghasiram is seated in a fellow Brahmin's house consoling him on the death of his wife by quoting from the *Bhagavad Gita*: 'Just as a person sheds his tattered clothes and puts on fresh ones, so one's soul abandons a decayed body and finds abode in a fresh one.' That is what has happened to the young man's dead wife, says Ghasiram, so why be sad? Follow his own example and acquire a new wife. Then, pausing in his sanctimonious discourse, Ghasiram catches sight of Dukhi squatting obediently in the road nearby, waiting to speak to him. Some minutes before, Ghasiram had despatched the *Chamar* to chop a trunk of wood the size and density of a boulder. Now he asks him, without preliminaries, 'Have you chopped wood?'

The thoughtless cruelty of this casual inquiry precisely defines the gulf between the two of them: Ghasiram the twice-born and Dukhi the *Chamar*, whom Ghasiram regards as little better than the animals he skins. It is Ray's singular achievement in *Deliverance* that he can make us feel the brutal strength of this symbiosis without allowing us even a single crumb of the usual comfort – not even a hint that this hierarchy may not endure for ever.

A.R.

Deliverance (Sadgati) was first broadcast on Doordarshan, the national television service in India, on 25 April 1982. The cast included:

DUKHI	Om Puri
JHURIA	Smita Patil
DHANIA	Richa Mishra
GHASIRAM	Mohan Agashe
LAKSHMI	Gita Siddharth
THE GOND	Bhaialal Hedao

Producer	Doordarshan, Government of India
Screenplay	Satyajit Ray, from a short story by Prem Chand
Lighting Cameraman	Soumendu Roy
Editor	Dulal Dutta
Art Director	Ashok Bose
Musical score	Satyajit Ray

CHARACTERS

DUKHI, a *Chamar*
JHURIA, Dukhi's wife
DHANIA, Dukhi's daughter
GHASIRAM, a Brahmin
LAKSHMI, Ghasiram's wife
THE GOND

A *CHAMAR* SETTLEMENT. DUKHI'S SHACK. MORNING
*The camera holds on the tiled roof of the shack. A goatskin lies spread
on it. The three main titles appear over the shot. At the end of titles
the camera pulls back and* JHURIA *enters the shot with a pitcher of
water on her head. She puts down the pitcher, looks around, and
calls out.*
JHURIA: Dhania! Dhania!
> (DHANIA *is seen to be playing with two other children and a
> small goat on the road in front of the shack. She looks up at her
> mother.*)

Where has your father gone?
DHANIA: To cut grass.
JHURIA: Cut grass? Now?
> (JHURIA, *puzzled, goes off to look for her husband. She finds
> him in a green patch on the edge of the settlement.* DUKHI *is
> indeed cutting grass.* JHURIA *stands looking over the fence.*)

What's the matter? Have you forgotten?
> (DUKHI *doesn't pay any attention to his wife.*)

Weren't you supposed to go to the Brahmin's this morning?
> (DUKHI *now turns round.*)

DUKHI: I can't go empty-handed, can I?
JHURIA: That grass is meant for him?
DUKHI: Who else? You go home and mind your own business.
  Think about what he's going to sit on.
JHURIA: Won't he sit on a cot?
DUKHI: Not on ours, surely.
JHURIA: We can borrow one from the headman.
DUKHI: Are you crazy? They won't let a coal out of their house
  to light your fire with – and they'll lend us a cot?
JHURIA: So?
DUKHI: Tell Dhania to break off some mohwa leaves. Make a
  mat with them.
JHURIA: Very well.
DUKHI: And we'll have to offer him some provisions too.
JHURIA: We'll need a plate for that.
DUKHI: Make a plate with mohwa leaves. They're holy.
> (DUKHI *has finished cutting grass and gets up with the bundle.*

85

He suddenly has a fainting fit, drops the bundle, and holds on to his wife for support. JHURIA *is anxious.*)

JHURIA: What happened?

    (DUKHI *takes a few seconds to recover.*)

    You felt dizzy, didn't you?

DUKHI: I'll be all right.

    (*He goes off towards his shack,* JHURIA *following.*)

    Take the Gond's daughter, go to the grocer's and bring back all the things we need.

JHURIA: What things?

DUKHI: Two pounds of flour, a pound of rice, half a pound of gram, a quarter of ghee, salt and turmeric. Will you remember?

JHURIA: Oh, yes.

DUKHI: Repeat what I said.

JHURIA: Two pounds of rice . . .

    (DUKHI *stops and turns reprovingly towards his wife.*)

DUKHI: Two pounds of *flour*!

    (JHURIA *repeats meekly.*)

JHURIA: Two pounds of flour.

DUKHI: A pound of rice. Repeat.

JHURIA: A pound of rice.

DUKHI: Half a pound of gram.

JHURIA: Half a pound of gram.

DUKHI: A quarter of ghee.

JHURIA: A quarter of ghee.

DUKHI: Salt and turmeric.

JHURIA: Salt and turmeric.

DUKHI: And put four annas at the edge of the leaf. Don't touch anything.

(They have reached the shack. DUKHI *throws down the bundle from his head.* JHURIA *suddenly has a thought.)*

JHURIA: Listen. Don't go today. Go tomorrow. You've only just recovered from fever . . .

DUKHI: I should have gone earlier. It's the fever which has delayed me. Don't worry. I'll be all right.

*(*DUKHI *goes into the shack.* DHANIA *comes in carrying the young goat.)*

Dhania!

*(*DHANIA *turns.)*

Come here.

*(*DHANIA *comes and stands facing her father.* DUKHI *gives her an affectionate pat on the head.)*

D'you know who's coming here today?

*(*DHANIA *nods.)*

Who?

DHANIA: Panditji.

DUKHI: And d'you know why he's coming?

*(*DHANIA *is too shy to answer.)*

Listen, go and break off some mohwa leaves and bring them here. You'll make a mat and a plate for the Brahmin. Bring a lot of leaves.

*(*DHANIA *sets off, but is called back by* DUKHI.*)*

And stay in the house after you're back. The Brahmin may want to see you.

*(*DUKHI *turns to go. He takes up the bundle of grass and prepares to leave.* JHURIA *has just brought out a plate with some food on it and a glass of water.)*

JHURIA: Going without eating? You had nothing to eat this morning.

DUKHI: I must hurry, or I'll miss him.

> (DUKHI *has already gone out of the shack. He is now surrounded by a herd of cows on its way to the pasture.*)

JHURIA: What if you get another dizzy spell on the way?

DUKHI: (*Raising his voice above the cowbells*) Keep everything ready here.

GHASIRAM THE BRAHMIN'S HOUSE

GHASIRAM, *freshly bathed, sits before a mirror carefully drawing sandalwood lines on his forehead. Then with vermilion he draws a red circle in the middle of the white lines.*

VILLAGE

DUKHI *on his way to the Brahmin's house carrying the grass on his head.*

GHASIRAM'S HOUSE

GHASIRAM *performs his* puja, *ringing a bell and waving a lamp in a circular motion before the deity.* DUKHI *passes a huge image of Ravana in the village square of the Brahmin quarter. He stops in front of the house. The ringing of the bell continues.* DUKHI *now makes his way to the back of the house. The back door is open.* DUKHI *enters. The sound of the bell is louder now.* DUKHI *comes to the door of the courtyard, puts down the bundle of grass, sits on his haunches and waits for the* puja *to be over.*

CHAMAR SETTLEMENT

DHANIA *tears off leaves from a mohwa tree.*

GHASIRAM'S HOUSE

The ringing stops. DUKHI *stiffens. The Brahmin may come out any moment now.* GHASIRAM *comes into the courtyard, walks across.*

DUKHI: Maharaj!

> (GHASIRAM *stops and turns.* DUKHI *prostrates himself on the veranda of the courtyard.* GHASIRAM'S *wife* LAKSHMI, *the* Panditayin, *also reacts from the inner veranda. She has been grinding spices.*)

GHASIRAM: Who is it?

DUKHI: Dukhi, Maharaj. I have come to see you.

GHASIRAM: What for?

DUKHI: We're arranging for our daughter's betrothal. If you could come and help us fix an auspicious date.

GHASIRAM: Now?

DUKHI: I've kept everything ready, Maharaj.

(GHASIRAM's *ten-year-old son* MOTI *has just come out with his schoolbooks and stops on the veranda to find out what's going on.* GHASIRAM *shouts at him.*)

GHASIRAM: What are you standing there for? You want to be late for school again?

(MOTI *meekly steps down from the veranda and ambles off.* GHASIRAM *turns to* DUKHI *again.*)

You think I'm free to go anywhere people want me to go?

DUKHI: Oh no, Maharaj, I know you have hardly any time to breathe. But I can't fix my daughter's betrothal without your help.

GHASIRAM: See there's a broom lying there.

DUKHI: Yes, Maharaj.

GHASIRAM: Sweep that veranda clean. I'll come when I'm free.

DUKHI: Maharaj, where shall I put this grass down?

GHASIRAM: Put it in the cowshed.

DUKHI: Very good, Maharaj.

(GHASIRAM *goes back into the house.*)

(DUKHI *takes the bundle of grass into the cowshed and does as told. Then he comes back to the front of the house, picks up the broom and starts to sweep.*)

THE GROCER'S SHOP

The old grocer hands a small girl some provisions and turns to JHURIA *and* THE GOND'S DAUGHTER.

GROCER: Yes?

(THE GOND'S DAUGHTER *turns to* JHURIA.)

GOND'S DAUGHTER: Well, tell him.

JHURIA: Two pounds of flour, a pound of rice, half of gram, a quarter of ghee, salt and turmeric.

GROCER: Hm. Two pounds of rice –

(JHURIA *giggles.*)

JHURIA: No, no! Two pounds of *flour*.

GHASIRAM'S HOUSE
DUKHI *finishes sweeping the front of the house and calls out.*
DUKHI: Maharaj!
    (GHASIRAM *has been drinking* bhang *out of a* lota, *sitting on a* charpoy.)
I have cleaned the veranda, Maharaj.
GHASIRAM: Now listen – there's a storeroom across the street, out in front. You'll find a pile of husk lying there. Take it out and put it in the cowshed.
DUKHI: Very good, Maharaj.
    (DUKHI *turns to go, but* GHASIRAM *calls out again.*)
GHASIRAM: And listen –
    (DUKHI *stops and turns.*)
After that I want you to chop wood for me. You'll find a log lying below the banyan tree outside. I want it chopped up in small bits. Understand?
    (DUKHI *is silent.*)
DUKHI: Yes, Maharaj.
    (DUKHI *makes his way to the storeroom. There is an immense pile of husk. An empty sack lies alongside.* DUKHI *fills the sack and hoists it on his shoulder. Then he crosses the wide street, goes in through the back door, dumps the husk, and starts back again.*)

DUKHI'S SHACK
DHANIA *has brought the mohwa leaves and calls out to her mother.*
DHANIA: Mohwa leaves, Mother.
    (JHURIA *is sweeping.*)
JHURIA: Put them down there.
DHANIA: Shall I make the plate?
JHURIA: Can you do it?
DHANIA: Why not?
JHURIA: All right, but do it properly. See that there are no holes, or the grain will trickle through.
    (DHANIA *gets down happily to making a plate with the leaves.*)

COWSHED
DUKHI *dumps the second pile of husk in the fodder bin and starts back.*

GHASIRAM'S HOUSE

A veranda on the street side. GHASIRAM *is seated with two other Brahmins. One of them,* LOKNATH, *a young, sheepish-looking character, has had a bereavement, and* GHASIRAM *is consoling him by quoting from the* Gita.

GHASIRAM: As the Lord Krishna says in the Gita: (*Quotes in Sanskrit*) 'Just as a person sheds his tattered clothes and puts on fresh ones, so one's soul abandons a decayed body and finds abode in a fresh one.' So you must remember that although your wife is dead, her soul lives.

LOKNATH: I find that a most consoling thought, Maharaj.

GHASIRAM: So why be sad? You're still young. Take another wife. Nowhere does it say in the Scriptures that you cannot marry again.

(DUKHI *comes and waits, squatting on the street, facing* GHASIRAM, *who continues with his discourse to the afflicted Brahmin.*)

Look at me. My present wife is my third. My first wife died seven months after marriage. A year later I married again. In three years I lost my second wife too. A snake bit her. A krait. On the ankle. Died in two hours.

(*The other two Brahmins look sympathetic.*

DUKHI *still waits to draw* GHASIRAM's *attention.*)

Two years later I married for the third time. You may suffer bereavement but life does not stop. It goes on.

(GHASIRAM *notices* DUKHI.)

Have you chopped wood?

DUKHI: Where is the axe, Maharaj?

GHASIRAM: Look in the storeroom.

DUKHI: Very good, Maharaj.

(GHASIRAM *pauses for* DUKHI *to go, then turns to* LOKNATH *again.*)

GHASIRAM: It is our sacred duty to marry and procreate. You have no son by your first wife, do you? Then it is your duty to marry again and keep alive your lineage.

(GHASIRAM *concludes with a smile.*)

THE LOG OF WOOD BY THE BANYAN TREE

DUKHI's *shadow falls on it. It is a massive trunk, and* DUKHI *regards it with foreboding. He walks around it, looking for the best position from which to attack it.*

He finds one and gets ready. Gripping the axe, he raises it over his head and brings it down on the log. The blade glances off. He brings it down again. Again the blade glances off. A third time the blade glances off. He tries once more. DUKHI *now examines the edge of the blade and looks around for something to use as a hone. He spots a stone slab lying nearby. He scoops some water from a puddle, wets the stone with it and starts rubbing the blade of the axe against it. He walks over to the log and attacks it with fresh vigour.*

A GOND *passing by slows down to have a look.* DUKHI *is trying hard but not to much effect. The* GOND, *a middle-aged man of grave countenance, walks up.*

GOND: Do you know how to chop wood?

(DUKHI *stops and turns towards the* GOND.)

DUKHI: I'm used to cutting grass, brother, not to chopping wood.

GOND: Then why wear yourself out for nothing?

DUKHI: Maharaj's orders. I'm taking him home to find an auspicious date for my daughter's betrothal.

GOND: So that's why he makes you chop wood?

DUKHI: I could do it too. It's just that I had no time to take any food this morning.

GOND: Can't he feed you even if he doesn't pay you? Ask him for some food.

DUKHI: I'm asking a favour, how can I ask for food?

GOND: Then whack away! Whack away!

(*The* GOND *walks away in disgust.*)

DUKHI: I could tackle it better if I had a smoke. It's not that I have no strength in my arms.

(*The* GOND *stops and turns.*)

GOND: Don't you have tobacco?

(DUKHI *shakes his head.*)

Come with me then.

DUKHI: Where?

GOND: Drop the axe and come with me.

(DUKHI *decides to go with the* GOND.)

DUKHI'S SHACK

JHURIA *has nearly finished making the mat.* DHANIA *is working on the plate.*

JHURIA: I wonder what's taking them so long. Dhania, go and take a look.

(DHANIA *does as told, but the road is empty.*)
DHANIA: There's no one coming, Mother.

THE GOND'S SHACK
DUKHI *stands waiting outside. The* GOND *comes out with pipe and tobacco.*
GOND: Sorry, there's no fire.
DUKHI: I'll get fire from the Brahmin's wife.
GOND: Carry on, then. I'll drop by later.
  (DUKHI *starts to walk back.*)

GHASIRAM'S HOUSE
GHASIRAM *has sat down to his meal.* LAKSHMI *sits near by with a fan.* DUKHI's *voice is heard.*
DUKHI: (*Off-screen*) Maharaj!
  (*Both* GHASHIRAM *and* LAKSHMI *react.*)
LAKSHMI: Why is that man back again?
GHASIRAM: He wants me to come to his house to fix a date for his daughter's betrothal.
LAKSHMI: Now, in the middle of the day?

93

GHASIRAM: I've asked him to do some work. Let him finish that first.

LAKSHMI: What work?

GHASIRAM: Chopping wood.

(*We see* DUKHI *now.*)

DUKHI: If I could get some fire to light this pipe.

(*Inside,* LAKSHMI *turns to her husband, her eyebrows raised.*)

LAKSHMI: He's asking for fire now!

GHASIRAM: Why don't you give him some?

(LAKSHMI *flies into a temper.*)

LAKSHMI: You seem to have forgotten all about caste rules. Chamars, washermen, bird-shooters come walking in as if they owned the house.

(LAKSHMI *has raised her voice, and* DUKHI *can hear her from outside.*)

(*Off-screen*) You'd think it was an inn, not a decent Hindu's house. Tell him to get out or I'll scorch his face with a firebrand.

(DUKHI *hangs his head in shame.*

Inside, GHASIRAM *continues to implore his wife.*)

GHASIRAM: He's doing our work, isn't he? If you had a labourer to do it, you'd have to pay him at least a rupee. Why don't you give him some fire?

(LAKSHMI *hoists herself up on her feet.*)

LAKSHMI: If he ever comes into the house again, I'll give him the coals in his face.

(DUKHI *stands fidgeting guiltily on the veranda.*

LAKSHMI *comes out holding the coals in a pair of tongs. With her veil drawn over her face, she flings the coals towards* DUKHI. *One of them hits* DUKHI *on the foot and he winces.* LAKSHMI *has gone back into the house.* DUKHI *raises his voice and apologizes while he puts the live coals into the* chillum.)

DUKHI: Forgive me, Mother. It was very wrong of me to come inside the house. It's because we're such fools that we get kicked about.

(*Inside,* LAKSHMI *reacts to* DUKHI's *apology. She seems to soften a bit.* GHASIRAM *continues to eat. She seems to ponder for a while.*)

LAKSHMI: Has the Chamar had anything to eat?

GHASIRAM: Perhaps not. He's been here since morning.

LAKSHMI: How can he chop wood on an empty stomach?
GHASIRAM: Why don't you give him something to eat?
LAKSHMI: What?
GHASIRAM: I don't know. Is there anything left over?
LAKSHMI: There are a couple of chapatis.
GHASIRAM: A couple? Hardly enough for a Chamar. Those fellows eat a lot.
    (LAKSHMI *gives up.*)
LAKSHMI: Then let him go hungry. I can't go cooking in this hot weather.

THE LOG OF WOOD
DUKHI *has sat down on the log to smoke. He takes a few long pulls, puts down the pipe, picks up the axe and straightens up.*

GHASIRAM'S HOUSE
GHASIRAM *washes his mouth.*
    The sound of chopping wood begins again.

GHASIRAM *goes and lies down on the* charpoy *with a fan in his hand.*

THE LOG OF WOOD
DUKHI *has attacked the log with renewed energy. His body glistens with sweat. Some marks have appeared on the wood – the result of a dozen vigorous whacks.* DUKHI *stops and looks at the marks. They seem to give him hope that he will be able to tackle it.*

After half a dozen more whacks DUKHI *has to stop again. It is obvious that many more will be needed before the wood yields.* DUKHI *seems to be possessed by a great stubbornness. He starts again, muttering under his breath.*

DUKHI: You son-of-a-bitch, I'll see you split even if I have to give my life for it.

GHASIRAM'S BEDROOM
GHASIRAM *is asleep on his cot. A gentle snore issues from his nostrils. The sound of chopping wood is heard off-screen.*

THE LOG OF WOOD
DUKHI: To hell with you!
   (*After a few more vigorous whacks,* DUKHI *suddenly loses his patience. Muttering an oath, he flings the axe away. The axe flies towards the road, and a Brahmin passer-by,* BHAGWANDAS, *has to duck to avoid having his head chopped off. He stares aghast at* DUKHI. DUKHI *runs up and retrieves the axe. He is profusely apologetic.*)
Forgive me, sir. It slipped out of my hand. It'll never happen again.
   (*Still speechless and with a look of horror,* BHAGWANDAS *steps back. He meets up with another* BRAHMIN *on his way to the well.*)
BRAHMIN: What's the matter, Bhagwandas?
BHAGWANDAS: (*Indicates to stay back*) He threw an axe at me.
BRAHMIN: Who?
BHAGWANDAS: That Chamar. Don't come this way.
   (DUKHI, *back near the log of wood, has heard this exchange. He suddenly feels forlorn. He drops the axe and flops down at the foot of the ancient tree. He glances at the log. It looks as indomitable as ever. He turns his eyes away. He seems suddenly*

overcome with a great weariness. His lips tremble. His eyes fill with tears. He gives way to a fit of sobbing.)

DUKHI'S SHACK
JHURIA *has fallen asleep on the veranda. The provisions for the Brahmin lie neatly arranged on the leaf plate beside her.* DHANIA *plays hop scotch before the shack, gets tired, goes to the road to see if her father is returning. Seeing no sign of* DUKHI, *she goes back to her play.*

GHASIRAM'S HOUSE
GHASIRAM *stirs, opens his eyes, glances at the clock. It is 2.21 p.m. There is silence all around but for a lone dove which calls incessantly from somewhere.* GHASIRAM *leaves his bed. His wife is asleep. He goes out, holding his sacred thread, to see what* DUKHI *is doing.*

THE LOG OF WOOD
DUKHI *has fallen asleep leaning against the trunk of the banyan tree.*
GHASIRAM *looks at the log. No splitting has been done yet.*
GHASIRAM: Have you come to snooze?
(DUKHI *wakes up with a start.*)
Dukhia?!
(DUKHI *gets up on his feet, has another dizzy spell, and has to hold on to the tree to avoid toppling over.*)
What's the matter?
DUKHI: I had nothing to eat this morning, Maharaj.
GHASIRAM: So what? Finish your work, go home and eat all you like. The wood's lying there just the way it was. So if you don't find an auspicious day for your daughter's marriage, don't blame me . . . Come on – get going.
(DUKHI *staggers to his feet weakly, picks up the axe and starts again. The* GOND *is back and watches from the gate. So does* MOTI. DUKHI *gives a few feeble whacks.*)
You seem to have no strength in your arms? Hit hard! Hard!
(DUKHI *calls up all his energy and begins to hit harder.*)
That's it. That's the way. Don't stop until you've split it. Yes, that's the way.
(GHASIRAM *goes away.* DUKHI *now whacks away as if possessed by a demonic strength.* MOTI *watches* DUKHI *raining blows on the log.* DUKHI *goes on ceaselessly, using the last ounce*

97

of energy, whack after whack, his body bathed in sweat, his veins standing out, his eyes starting out of their sockets. A tremendous blow makes the axe stick in the wood and the next moment – DUKHI falls on his face. The axe lies embedded in the log. DUKHI's body remains inert.

MOTI walks up close, looks on for a while, then senses something is wrong. He runs away.)

GHASIRAM'S BEDROOM
GHASIRAM *has got back to bed for another nap.* MOTI *comes charging in.*
MOTI: Daddy, Daddy, the Chamar is dead.
GHASIRAM: What?
MOTI: The Chamar's dead. He's fallen on his face by the log.
(GHASIRAM scrambles into his chappals, gives his son a slap and goes out to investigate.)
GHASIRAM: Must have fallen asleep again.

THE LOG OF WOOD
Before setting eyes on the body, he calls out.
Dukhiya, dozed off again, have you?
(Then GHASIRAM sees the situation. He orders MOTI away to play.)
What are you standing there for? Go and play. Go to Tulsi's house. Go on!
(GHASIRAM takes a closer look at DUKHI, while keeping his distance. DUKHI looks what he is – a dead man. GHASIRAM goes white as a sheet. There is now no doubt in his mind that DUKHI is dead. Seized with panic, he runs back into the house.
The GOND, who has seen everything, moves forward.)

GHASIRAM'S BEDROOM
GHASIRAM *shakes his wife out of her sleep.*
GHASIRAM: Listen. Disaster.
LAKSHMI: What d'you mean?
GHASIRAM: Dukhi is dead.
LAKSHMI: Who's Dukhi?
GHASIRAM: Dukhi the Chamar.
LAKSHMI: But wasn't he chopping wood?
GHASIRAM: He died chopping wood.

LAKSHMI: Are you sure he's not asleep?

GHASIRAM: You think I don't know a dead man when I see one?

LAKSHMI: But what are you so jumpy about? (*She ponders for a moment.*) Go to the Chamar's colony and tell them to come and take the corpse away.

GHASIRAM: But the trouble is, you see –

LAKSHMI: What are you mumbling for? He was chopping wood and died. He must have been ill. Maybe he had fever. Some people die in their sleep, don't they? After all, you didn't know that he would die.

GHASIRAM: No, of course not.

LAKSHMI: Well, don't sit there. Go.

THE LOG OF WOOD

The GOND *is kneeling by* DUKHI. *He makes sure that the* Chamar *is dead. He gives a contemptuous glance in the direction of* GHASI-RAM's *house.*

GOND: Holy man! God incarnate!

(*The* GOND *gets up and makes off with quick steps. On the road, the Brahmin* BHAGWANDAS *stands looking suspiciously at* DUKHI's *inert body. He turns to the* GOND *who is crossing the road.*)

BHAGWANDAS: What's the matter with him?

GOND: He's dead.

BHAGWANDAS: Who is he?

GOND: Dukhi the Chamar.

(*The* GOND *is gone.*)

BHAGWANDAS: (*Horrified*) The Chamar is dead!

THE CHAMAR SETTLEMENT

A crowd has gathered to listen to the GOND.

GOND: He died while chopping wood. That Brahmin forced him to work. So he is responsible. I know because I saw everything with my own eyes. He will come here. He will ask you to remove the corpse. Don't touch the corpse or you'll be in trouble with the police. It's a police case, and the guilty one is the Brahmin.

(JHURIA *comes out of her shack. She senses something is wrong. The* GOND *leaves, passing* GHASIRAM *on his way to the* Chamar *settlement.* GHASIRAM *looks hesitant, but he musters up enough courage to address the* Chamars.)

99

GHASIRAM: Listen to me, brothers. A little while ago, Dukhi died near my house.

(JHURIA *slowly approaches the group of* Chamars. *Cowbells are heard again.*)

I was about to come with him to his house when he died quite suddenly. The question is, how long is the corpse going to be there?

JHURIA: Oh God! I knew it. I knew there was something wrong.

(*She falls to the ground as a herd of cattle low behind her. Two women try to console her.*)

What'll happen to me now?

(*Above the wailing* GHASIRAM *persists.*)

GHASIRAM: If you could do something about . . .

(*The* Chamars *don't budge. They just keep looking at* GHASIRAM. GHASIRAM *loses his nerve and starts pacing back.* JHURIA *is still wailing.* DHANIA *sniffles. A rumble of thunder is heard.*)

EXTERIOR OF GHASIRAM'S HOUSE

A crowd has gathered on the road, and is commenting on the event.

GHASIRAM *is seen approaching his house. The crowd, all Brahmins, walk up to him.* BHAGWANDAS *speaks.*

BHAGWANDAS: This is a serious matter, Panditji. Until the corpse is removed, we can't use this road to go to the well. How long can we do without water?

GHASIRAM: I've just been to the Chamar settlement and told them. They'll be here presently. You go home now and come back in an hour. Go on home.

INSIDE GHASIRAM'S HOUSE

Thunder. LAKSHMI *pulls down a sari from the clothes line and turns to her husband.* GHASIRAM *comes in, shakes his head and lies down on the* charpoy *again.*

LAKSHMI: What happened?

GHASIRAM: They won't listen.

LAKSHMI: What do you mean?

GHASIRAM: They won't remove the corpse.

LAKSHMI: Nonsense. They don't expect us to remove it, do they?

GHASIRAM: Don't ask me.

(*He turns to the wall.*)

LAKSHMI: What did you tell them?

GHASIRAM: I told them what had to be told. That Dukhi is dead, go and remove his dead body . . . They just turned a deaf ear and looked at me with red eyes. I had to come away.

LAKSHMI: Now it's started raining, and the corpse is still lying there.

THE LOG OF WOOD

Outside, DUKHI's *dead body is pelted by rain.* JHURIA *comes, soaked to the skin. She walks up and turns over the body of her husband. Wailing, she shakes the body.*

JHURIA: Open your eyes! . . . Open your eyes! . . . What a curse this is! Our only daughter just about to be married! I must go and fetch the Brahmin, he said. Who knew he would never return? How could you be so cruel? Didn't you once think of me and what would happen to me?

(JHURIA *now turns towards* GHASIRAM's *house.*)

Maharaj!

INSIDE GHASIRAM'S HOUSE
LAKSHMI *reacts to the cry. She runs up and bolts the front door.*

OUTSIDE GHASIRAM'S HOUSE
JHURIA *comes running up towards the front door in the pouring rain.*
JHURIA: Maharaj, you made him chop wood – made him work
   so hard – when he had fever only the other day. He had
   nothing to eat this morning – he had no strength – yet you
   made him work. What harm had he done you that you were
   so cruel?
   (JHURIA *falls on the doorstep and starts banging on the door,
   weeping.*)

THE LOG OF WOOD. NIGHT
It is raining heavily. DUKHI'S *body, now lying face up, is lit by
flashes of lightning.*

GHASIRAM'S BEDROOM
LAKSHMI *sits on the bed while* GHASIRAM *paces up and down.*
LAKSHMI: I don't know why you had to ask him to split wood.
GHASIRAM: I didn't know he'd had nothing to eat. I told you to
   give him some food.
LAKSHMI: You told me? It was I who told you.
GHASIRAM: But you refused to give him any food and now you
   blame me.
LAKSHMI: A poor starving man and you made him work so hard.
GHASIRAM: Don't tell me people who work hard all die.
LAKSHMI: What happens if the police come to know?
GHASIRAM: You expect the police to be out in this weather?
LAKSHMI: The corpse will start stinking soon. They won't
   remove the corpse, and you won't find anyone to do it for
   you.
GHASIRAM: Stop jabbering and let me think.
   (*He stops pacing.*)
   (*To himself*) Let me think . . . let me think . . .

THE LOG OF WOOD. DAWN THE NEXT DAY
*The rain has stopped, but there are puddles all around, and water
drips from the leaves of the trees.*

Close-up of DUKHI's *legs. One stiff leg is lifted with the help of a stout, bent twig and a noose slipped around the ankle. It binds tightly as the rope is pulled.*

GHASIRAM *grips the rope. He has to exert all his strength to haul the corpse towards the field beyond.*

FIELD

We hear a loud puffing and panting, and GHASIRAM *enters the shot silhouetted against the sky, dragging the stiff corpse and nearly collapsing in the process. He slips and stumbles in the slush but carries on with a grim and somewhat comical determination. He grows smaller as he recedes from the camera, the corpse in tow.*

Nearly out of breath, GHASIRAM *dumps the corpse in a spot used for dumping animals – their bones lie all around. This is* DUKHI's *final resting place. We hear a cock crowing, heralding the beginning of another day.*

THE LOG OF WOOD

Now we see GHASIRAM, *his* dhoti *still wet from his bath. He chants prayers and sprinkles holy water on the spot where* DUKHI *died.*

We see the log with the axe sticking out of it, the holy water cleansing it and the place around of all impurity.

GHASIRAM *moves out of the shot, still sprinkling and chanting. The dawn chorus begins.*

We stay on the log of wood and the axe, while the end Titles appear over them.

SADGATI (DELIVERANCE)

by Prem Chand
Translated by David Rubin

Dukhi the *Chamar* (tanner) was sweeping in front of his door while Jhuria, his wife, plastered the floor with cow-dung. When they both found a moment to rest from their work Jhuria said, 'Aren't you going to the Brahmin to ask him to come? If you don't he's likely to go off somewhere.'

'Yes, I'm going,' Dukhi said, 'but we have to think about what he's going to sit on.'

'Can't we find a cot somewhere? You could borrow one from the village headman's wife.'

'Sometimes the things you say are really aggravating! The people in the headman's house give me a cot? They won't even let a coal out of their house to light your fire with, so are they going to give me a cot? Even when they're where I can go and talk to them if I ask for a pot of water I won't get it, so who'll give me a cot? A cot isn't like the things we've got – cow-dung fuel or chaff or wood that anybody who wants can pick up and carry off. You'd better wash our own cot and set it out – in this hot weather it ought to be dry by the time he comes.'

'He won't sit on our cot,' Jhuria said. 'You know what a stickler he is about religion and doing things according to the rule.'

A little worried, Dukhi said, 'Yes, that's true. I'll break off some mohwa leaves and make a mat for him, that will be the thing. Great gentlemen eat off mohwa leaves, they're holy. Hand me my stick and I'll break some off.'

'I'll make the mat, you go to him. But we'll have to offer him some food he can take home and cook, won't we? I'll put it in my dish –'

'Don't commit any such sacrilege!' Dukhi said. 'If you do, the offering will be wasted and the dish broken. Baba will just pick up the dish and dump it. He flies off the handle very fast, and when he's in a rage he doesn't even spare his wife, and he beat his son so badly that even now the boy goes around with a broken hand. So we'll put the offering on a leaf too. Just don't touch it. Take Jhuri the Gond's daughter to the village merchant and bring back all the things we need. Let it be a complete offering

105

– a full two pounds of flour, a half of rice, a quarter of gram, an eighth of ghee, salt, turmeric, and four annas at the edge of the leaf. If you don't find the Gond girl then get the woman who runs the parching oven, beg her to go if you have to. Just don't touch anything because that will be a great wrong.'

After these instructions Dukhi picked up his stick, took a big bundle of grass and went to make his request to the Pandit. He couldn't go empty-handed to ask a favour of the Pandit; he had nothing except the grass for a present. If Panditji ever saw him coming without an offering, he'd shout abuse at him from far away.

2

Pandit Ghasiram was completely devoted to God. As soon as he awoke he would busy himself with his rituals. After washing his hands and feet at eight o'clock he would begin the real ceremony of worship, the first part of which consisted of the preparation of *bhang*. After that he would grind sandalwood paste for half an hour, then with a straw he would apply it to his forehead before the mirror. Between two lines of sandalwood paste he would draw a red circle. Then on his chest and arms he would draw designs of perfect circles. After this he would take out the image of the Lord, bathe it, apply the sandalwood to it, deck it with flowers, perform the ceremony of lighting the lamp before it and ringing a little bell. At ten o'clock he'd rise from his devotions and after a drink of the *bhang* go outside where a few clients would have gathered: such was the reward for his piety; this was his crop to harvest.

Today when he came from the shrine in his house he saw Dukhi the Untouchable tanner sitting there with a bundle of grass. As soon as he caught sight of him Dukhi stood up, prostrated himself on the ground, stood up again and folded his hands. Seeing the Pandit's glorious figure his heart was filled with reverence. How godly a sight! – a rather short, roly-poly fellow with a bald, shiny skull, chubby cheeks and eyes aglow with brahminical energy. The sandalwood markings bestowed on him the aspect of the gods. At the sight of Dukhi he intoned, 'What brings you here today, little Dukhi?'

Bowing his head, Dukhi said, 'I'm arranging Bitiya's betrothal.

Will Your Worship help us to fix an auspicious date? When can you find the time?'

'I have no time today,' Panditji said. 'But still, I'll manage to come toward evening.'

'No, Maharaj, please come soon. I've arranged everything for you. Where shall I set this grass down?'

'Put it down in front of the cow and if you'll just pick up that broom sweep it clean in front of the door,' Panditji said. 'Then the floor of the sitting room hasn't been plastered for several days so plaster it with cowdung. While you're doing that I'll be having my lunch, then I'll rest a bit and after that I'll come. Oh yes, you can split that wood too, and in the storeroom there's a little pile of hay – just take it out and put it into the fodder bin.'

Dukhi began at once to carry out the orders. He swept the doorstep, he plastered the floor. This took until noon. Panditji went off to have his lunch. Dukhi, who had eaten nothing since morning, was terribly hungry. But there was no way he could eat here. His house was a mile away – if he went to eat there Panditji would be angry. The poor fellow suppressed his hunger and began to split the wood. It was a fairly thick tree trunk on which a great many devotees had previously tried their strength and it was ready to match iron with iron in any fight. Dukhi, who was used to cutting grass and bringing it to the market, had no experience with cutting wood. The grass would bow its head before his sickle but now even when he brought the axe down with all his strength it didn't make a mark on the trunk. The axe just glanced off. He was drenched in sweat, panting, he sat down exhausted and got up again. He could scarcely lift his hands, his legs were unsteady, he couldn't straighten out his back. Then his vision blurred, he saw spots, he felt dizzy, but still he went on trying. He thought that if he could get a pipeful of tobacco to smoke then perhaps he might feel refreshed. This was a Brahmin village, and Brahmins didn't smoke tobacco at all like the low castes and Untouchables. Suddenly he remembered that there was a Gond living in the village too, surely he would have a pipeful. He set off at a run for the man's house at once, and he was in luck. The Gond gave him both pipe and tobacco, but he had no fire to light it with. Dukhi said, 'Don't worry about the fire, brother, I'll go to Panditji's house and ask him for a light, they're still cooking there.'

With this he took the pipe and came back and stood on the veranda of the Brahmin's house, and he said, 'Master, if I could get just a little bit of light I'll smoke this pipeful.'

Panditji was eating and his wife said, 'Who's that man asking for a light?'

'It's only that damned little Dukhi the tanner. I told him to cut some wood. The fire's lit, so go give him his light.'

Frowning, the Panditayin said, 'You've become so wrapped up in your books and astrological charts that you've forgotten all about caste rules. If there's a tanner or a washerman or a bird-shooter, why, he can just come walking right into the house as though he owned it. You'd think it was an inn and not a decent Hindu's house. Tell that good-for-nothing to get out or I'll scorch his face with a firebrand.'

Trying to calm her down, Panditji said, 'He's come inside – so what? Nothing that belongs to you has been stolen. The floor is clean, it hasn't been desecrated. Why not just let him have his light – he's doing our work, isn't he? You'd have to pay at least four annas if you hired some labourer to split it.'

Losing her temper, the Panditayin said, 'What does he mean coming into this house!'

'It was the son of a bitch's bad luck, what else?' the Pandit said.

'It's all right,' she said, 'this time I'll give him his fire but if he ever comes into the house again like that I'll give him the coals in his face.'

Fragments of this conversation reached Dukhi's ears. He repented: it was a mistake to come. She was speaking the truth – how could a tanner ever come into a Brahmin's house? These people were clean and holy, that was why the whole world worshipped them and respected them. A mere tanner was absolutely nothing. He had lived all his life in the village without understanding this before.

Therefore when the Pandit's wife came out bringing coals it was like a miracle from heaven. Folding his hands and touching his forehead to the ground he said, 'Panditayin, Mother, it was very wrong of me to come inside your house. Tanners don't have much sense – if we weren't such fools why would we get kicked so much?'

The Panditayin had brought the coals in a pair of tongs. From a few feet away, with her veil drawn over her face, she flung the coals toward Dukhi. Big sparks fell on his head and drawing back hastily he shook them out of his hair. To himself he said, 'This is what comes of dirtying a clean Brahmin's house. How quickly God pays you back for it! That's why everybody's afraid of Pandits. Everybody else gives up his money and never gets it back but who ever got any money out of a Brahmin? Anybody who tried would have his whole family destroyed and his legs would turn leprous.'

He went outside and smoked his pipe, then took up the axe and started to work again.

Because the sparks had fallen on him the Pandit's wife felt some pity for him. When the Pandit got up from his meal she said to him, 'Give this tanner something to eat, the poor fellow's been working for a long time, he must be hungry.'

Panditji considered this proposal entirely outside of the behaviour expected of him. He asked, 'Is there any bread?'

'There are a couple of pieces left over.'

'What's the good of two or three pieces for a tanner? Those people need at least a good two pounds.'

His wife put her hands over her ears. 'My, my, a good two pounds! Then let's forget about it.'

Majestically Panditji said, 'If there's some bran and husks mix them in flour and make a couple of pancakes. That'll fill the bastard's belly up. You can never fill up these low-caste people with good bread. Plain millet's what they need.'

'Let's forget the whole thing,' the Panditayin said, 'I'm not going to kill myself cooking in weather like this.'

3

When he took up the axe again after smoking his pipe, Dukhi found that with his rest the strength had to some extent come back into his arms. He swung the axe for about half an hour, then out of breath he sat down right there with his head in his hands.

In the meantime the Gond came. He said, 'Why are you wearing yourself out, old friend? You can whack it all you like but you won't split this trunk. You're killing yourself for nothing.'

Wiping the sweat from his forehead Dukhi said, 'I've still got to cart off a whole wagon-load of hay, brother.'

'Have you had anything to eat? Or are they just making you work without feeding you? Why don't you ask them for something?'

'How can you expect me to swallow a Brahmin's food, Chikhuri?'

'Swallowing it's no problem, you have to get it first. He sits in there and eats like a king and then has a nice little nap after he tells you you have to split his wood. The government officials may force you to work for them but they pay you something for it, no matter how little. This fellow's gone one better, calling himself a holy man.'

'Speak softly, brother, if they hear you we'll be in trouble.'

With that Dukhi went back to work and began to swing the axe. Chikhuri felt so sorry for him that he came and took the axe out of Dukhi's hands and worked with it for a good half-hour. But there was not even a crack in the wood. Then he threw the axe down and said, 'Whack it all you like but you won't split it, you're just killing yourself,' and he went away.

Dukhi began to think, 'Where did the Baba get hold of this trunk that can't be split? There's not even a crack in it so far. How long can I keep smashing into it? I've got a hundred things to do at home by now. In a house like mine there's no end to the work, something's always left over. But he doesn't worry about that. I'll just bring him his hay and tell him, "Baba, the wood didn't split. I'll come and finish it tomorrow."'

He lifted up the basket and began to bring the hay. From the storeroom to the fodder bin was no less than a quarter of a mile. If he'd really filled up the basket the work would have been quickly finished, but then who could have hoisted up the basket on his head? He couldn't raise a fully loaded basket, so he took just a little each time. It was four o'clock by the time he'd finished with the hay. At this time Pandit Ghasiram woke up, washed his hands and face, took some *paan* and came outside. He saw Dukhi asleep with the basket still on his head. He shouted, 'Arrey, Dukhia, sleeping? The wood's lying there just the way it was. What's taken you so long? You've used up the whole day just to bring in a little fistful of hay and then gone and fallen asleep! Pick up the axe and split that wood. You haven't even made a dent in it. So if you don't find an auspicious day for your daughter's marriage, don't blame me. This is why they say that as soon as an Untouchable gets a little food in his house he can't be bothered with you any more.'

Dukhi picked up the axe again. He completely forgot what he'd been thinking about before. His stomach was pasted against his backbone – he hadn't so much as eaten breakfast that morning, there wasn't any time. Just to stand up seemed an impossible task. His spirit flagged, but only for a moment. This was the Pandit, if he didn't fix an auspicious day the marriage would be a total failure. And that was why everybody respected the Pandits – everything depended on getting the right day set. He could ruin anybody he wanted to. Panditji came close to the log and standing there began to goad him. 'That's right, give it a real hard stroke, a real hard one. Come on now, really hit it! Don't you have any strength in your arm? Smash it, what's the point of standing there thinking about it? That's it, it's going to split, there's a crack in it.'

Dukhi was in a delirium; some kind of hidden power seemed to have come into his hands. It was as though fatigue, hunger, weakness, all had left him. He was astonished at his own strength. The axe-strokes descended one after another like lightning. He went on driving the axe in this state of intoxication until finally the log split down the middle. And Dukhi's hands let the axe drop. At the same moment, overcome with dizziness, he fell, the hungry, thirsty, exhausted body gave up.

Panditji called, 'Get up, just two or three more strokes. I want it in small bits.' Dukhi did not get up. It didn't seem proper to Pandit Ghasiram to insist now. He went inside, drank some *bhang*, emptied his bowels, bathed and came forth attired in full Pandit regalia. Dukhi was still lying on the ground. Panditji shouted, 'Well, Dukhi, are you going to just stay lying here? Let's go, I'm on my way to your house! Everything's set, isn't it?' But still Dukhi did not get up.

A little alarmed, Panditji drew closer and saw that Dukhi was absolutely stiff. Startled half out of his wits he ran into the house and said to his wife, 'Little Dukhi looks as though he's dead.'

Thrown into confusion Panditayin said, 'But hasn't he just been chopping wood?'

'He died right while he was splitting it. What's going to happen?'

Calmer, the Panditayin said, 'What do you mean what's going to happen? Send word to the tanners' settlement so they can come and take the corpse away.'

In a moment the whole village knew about it. It happened that except for the Gond house everyone who lived there was a Brahmin. People stayed off the road that went there. The only road to the well passed that way – how were they to get water? Who would come to draw water with a tanner's corpse nearby? One old woman said to Panditji, 'Why don't you get this body thrown away? Is anybody in the village going to be able to drink water or not?'

The Gond went from the village to the tanners' settlement and told everyone the story. 'Careful now!' he said. 'Don't go to get the body. There'll be a police investigation yet. It's no joke that somebody killed this poor fellow. The somebody may be a pandit, but just in his own house. If you move the body you'll get arrested too.'

Right after this Panditji arrived. But there was nobody in the settlement ready to carry the corpse away. To be sure, Dukhi's wife and daughter both went moaning to Panditji's door and tore their hair and wept. About a dozen other women went with them, and they wept too and they consoled them, but there was no man with them to bear away the body. Panditji threatened the tanners, he tried to wheedle them, but they were very mindful of the police and not one of them stirred. Finally Panditji went home disappointed.

4

At midnight the weeping and lamentation were still going on. It was hard for the Brahmins to fall asleep. But no tanner came to get the corpse, and how could a Brahmin lift up an Untouchable's body? It was expressly forbidden in the scriptures and no one could deny it.

Angrily the Panditayin said, 'Those witches are driving me out of my mind. And they're not even hoarse yet!'

'Let the hags cry as long as they want. When he was alive

nobody cared a straw about him. Now that he's dead everybody in the village is making a fuss about him.'

'The wailing of tanners is bad luck,' the Panditayin said.

'Yes, very bad luck.'

'And it's beginning to stink already.'

'Wasn't the bastard a tanner? Those people eat anything, clean or not, without worrying about it.'

'No sort of food disgusts them.'

'They're all polluted!'

Somehow or other they got through the night. But even in the morning no tanner came. They could still hear the wailing of the women. The stench was beginning to spread quite a bit.

Panditji got out a rope. He made a noose and managed to get it over the dead man's feet and drew it tight. Morning mist still clouded the air. Panditji grabbed the rope and began to drag it, and he dragged it until it was out of the village. When he got back home he bathed immediately, read out prayers to Durga for purification, and sprinkled Ganges water around the house.

Out there in the field the jackals and kites, dogs and crows were picking at Dukhi's body. This was the reward of a whole life of devotion, service and faith.

THE ALIEN

INTRODUCTION

The idea of *The Alien*, which Ray wrote in 1967, may come as a surprise to those who think of him as a humanist with his feet planted firmly in the social reality of Bengal past and present. Both these characteristics are in fact integral to *The Alien*, but they are combined with a penchant for magic and fantasy evident in some of Ray's films that are less known in the West, and especially in his highly successful Bengali writings, some of which he recently translated for publication abroad.*

The Alien is a small humanoid creature which lands its spaceship in a pond in the backwoods of a Bengali village like that, say, of *The Postmaster*. The first villager to encounter it is an orphan child called Haba who reminds us of Durga in *Pather Panchali*; he steals fruit from the neighbours' trees and gets beaten for it just as she did. Of all those who fall within the Alien's spell it is Haba who resembles it most closely. To quote Ray's description:

> [The Alien is] a cross between a gnome and a famished refugee child: large head, spindly limbs, a lean torso. Is it male or female? We don't know. What its form basically conveys is a kind of ethereal innocence, and it is difficult to associate either great evil or great power with it; yet a feeling of eeriness is there because of the resemblance to a sickly human child.

While Haba is delighted with his new friend, whom he first meets when it enters his dreams at night as he lies sleeping on the floor of his shack, the adult residents of the village are variously baffled, sceptical or suspicious. A miracle then convinces them, led by their priest, that the strange golden spire poking through the lotuses in the pond is really a submerged temple, and they begin to worship it: a conversion that seems only too convincing in the light of Ray's penetrating study of superstition, *The Goddess*.

It is the outsiders of the village who have other ideas. Mohan, a young journalist from Calcutta, who is staying there to write

---

* *Stories*, Secker and Warburg, 1987 (paperback edition Penguin, 1988).

about the changing face of the village, is the most rational of them; his mind ranges far and wide to explain the phenomenon and eventually connects it with some moving lights reported only days before in the night sky of Bengal. Joe Devlin, a 'can-do' American engineer from Montana is the most unmoved. He is in the village with pumping and drilling equipment and instructions to dig tube-wells, and these are his sole concern, except perhaps for the local Santhal women (precursors of the women who dance with abandon and defy the city types in *Days and Nights in the Forest*).

Devlin's boss, G. L. Bajoria, is the most unscrupulous. As he explains to Devlin he is not 'a rich man in a rich country' like J. D. Rockefeller but 'a rich man in a poor country . . . a sore thumb, and how can a sore thumb *ever* be a popular image, Mr Devlin?' The drilling of tube-wells improves his image; but even better for that purpose in a pious land is the building and restoring of temples. As soon as Bajoria catches sight of the golden spire in the pond he perceives its possibilities as 'the holiest place in India', with the bottom of the pond paved in marble and 'marble steps leading down from all four sides, and arches and pillars, and a little marble plaque to say: "salvaged and restored by Gaganlal Laxmikant Bajoria"!' And who better to pump out the water and fulfil his dream – for a consideration, of course – than Joe Devlin?

This character Bajoria, who was to have been played by Peter Sellers, is by no means improbable in India, where rich industrialists getting on in years but not in respectability have a habit of endowing religious foundations. The immensely wealthy Birla family, for instance, who, like Bajoria, belong to the Marwari community (along with the majority of film producers in Bengal today), were responsible for the 'restoration' of certain ruined old temples in Bengal which Ray loved, by having them painted pink during the 1960s. 'There is a little bit of Mr Birla in my Marwari,' Ray said with a smile in an interview in 1967.

The Alien itself has its own ideas for its visit to Earth of course, and for its spaceship; ideas which eventually open the eyes of Mohan the journalist and Devlin the engineer, though not those of the shrewd but superstitious Bajoria. Consumed by playful curiosity about the world in which it has just arrived, it hops invisibly around the village examining with its special powers of vision everything from the craters of the moon hanging in the sky to the circulation of blood in Haba's heart. It also gets up to much mischief: among its pranks are ripening a villager's corn overnight, making a mango-tree belonging to the meanest man in the village fruit at the wrong time of year, and causing an old man's corpse on its pyre to open its eyes under his grandson's nose.

The notion of the Alien is distinctly foreshadowed in two of Ray's earlier films, *The Philosopher's Stone (Parash Pathar)* and *Kanchenjungha*, as well as resembling in attitude the film he shot after *The Alien* was written, *The Adventures of Goopy and Bagha* – and I shall return to these; but its paternity is the story Ray wrote a few years before his screenplay, and that he refers to in his Preface. In this a benign alien creature descended upon a forest near an insignificant village in Bengal and made contact with one of its humblest residents, Banku Babu. Neither the character of that alien nor that of his friend was much developed, however; the bulk of the story consisted of amusing dialogues between other residents of the village about strange lights seen in the sky, and their taunting of the meek schoolmaster.

Ray's magazine for young people, in which this story appeared along with his illustrations of the alien creature, is called *Sandesh*, which means both 'Sweetmeat' and 'Information' or 'News'. It was first published and edited by Satyajit's grandfather from 1913 and then by his father until its collapse in 1926 after his father's death.

Looking at the superb fantasy and other drawings that appeared in the old *Sandesh*, reading the celebrated nonsense verse of Satyajit's father, and browsing through the articles on scientific and natural phenomena of all kinds – especially astronomical, since Satyajit's grandfather was a keen star-gazer – one realizes that *The Alien* is very much in a family tradition of whimsical speculation about the unknown. Both grandfather and father Ray had considerable experimental and theoretical scientific knowledge which they applied in developing their pioneering printing business. Satyajit, though less knowledgeable about science than they, retains their fascination with its mysteries.

One of his favourite authors as a child was Conan Doyle, whose widow granted one of Satyajit's great-uncles the right to translate Conan Doyle's works into Bengali, gratis. His scientist, Professor

Challenger, and his detective, Sherlock Holmes, have spawned two of Ray's most successful characters in print, Professor Shonku and Felu, known as Feluda by his teenage Watsonian sidekick (the suffix -da denoting respect in Bengal). Feluda is a particular favourite in Calcutta, where more than fifteen novellas about his exploits have now appeared, two of which Ray has filmed as *The Golden Fortress (Sonar Kella)* and *The Elephant God (Joi Baba Felunath)*.

Both Shonku and Feluda have an encyclopaedic curiosity about the world, and both keep open minds about its enigmas – like their creator, Ray. In fact Feluda is in many ways a better guide to Ray's personality than are his films. In *The Golden Fortress*, for instance, Feluda's interest is aroused by the kidnap of a young boy who claims to have a memory of treasure from a previous life spent somewhere in a golden fortress. Ray wrote the story after meeting a parapsychologist from a university in Rajasthan who had actually done research on a young boy with vivid recollections of a place he had never visited. Ray does not know whether he believes in reincarnation, but he says, 'There are so many examples of cases I think one should keep an open mind.'

The journalist in *The Alien* shares this same spirit of restless inquiry and wonder and is therefore the first to guess the true nature of the spaceship and its occupant. 'You know who discovered the zero?' he asks his baffled young wife. '*We* did – an unknown Indian – way back in the time of the Upanishads . . . *Shunya*! . . . It means space and it means zero – isn't that wonderful?'

Haba, the waif, in tune with nature but not with the villagers, is another kind of character typical of Ray's fiction. Both as a writer and as a director Ray has had a special rapport with solitary children; probably a consequence of his own solitary fatherless childhood in a household of adults. In one of Ray's best stories for instance, which is also an early one, a reserved young boy who hardly ever smiles becomes fascinated by ants and learns to understand their language. Everyone thinks he has become slightly mad and he is eventually sent to hospital. There, in a spotless room, two of his ant friends nevertheless gain entry. When the doctor arrives, he sees one of them and crushes it, but its comrade gets inside his white coat and bites him all over his arm – much to the satisfaction of the delighted boy. The way that the Alien pokes an ant-hill on its first night-time exploration of Earth, observes the swarming ants microscopically and listens to the sounds they make, clearly recalls this story.

The unworldly attitude of the Alien is mirrored in many of Ray's stories and novellas, certainly in Professor Shonku and Feluda, neither of whom seek money or fame for their work, but perhaps especially in Ray's affectionate portrayal of the struggling lower middle-class in Calcutta in stories like 'Patol Babu, Film Star' and 'Ashamanja Babu's Dog' (in his published collection in English translation). The second of these stories even contains an American character – a kind of cross between Devlin and Bajoria, with the former's suspicion of the supernatural and the latter's business instinct – who offers Ashamanja Babu an astronomical sum (by his standards) for his dog, because it is said to be able to laugh. The American's only condition is that the dog should demonstrate its remarkable talent in front of him. But when the dog unexpectedly does so, the American has no idea of the cause of its mirth. This is, of course, the American's unquestioning conviction that money can buy everything; and so Ashamanja Babu decides not to sell his wise pet.

The elderly clerk, Paresh Chandra Dutta, who finds the philosopher's stone that turns all it touches to gold while on his way home from the office one day, and uses it to shoot to the top of the tree, springs from the same source of humour as Ashamanja Babu. *The Philosopher's Stone*, the comedy Ray made in 1957, contains the germ of *The Alien*, Ray feels, although he was not conscious of this when he wrote either screenplay. In the 1957 film, which is based on a famous Bengali short story, Ray introduced many ideas of his own, one of which was a stroke of brilliance; instead of the little stone being found lying in the street, Ray had it fall from the sky in a shower of hailstones, rather as the Alien would later descend from the sky in its spaceship. The impact on society of both foreign bodies is similar too; they play havoc with it without really intending to. Dutta takes an innocent delight in the trappings of wealth – gold and jewellery galore, a big house, a splendid motor-car, a secretary with nothing to do, and honoured guest status at endless public functions where he distributes gold medals to all and sundry – but at no point does he harm anyone. Only when his secret gets out does everything go wrong for him; banks crash, crowds riot, the police close in and his life is reduced to its earlier ignominious penury – to his great relief. The Alien's mischievous miracles are comparably subversive, soon setting villager against villager, Bajoria against those he claims to be helping, and everyone (apart from Mohan) against the mysterious object in the pond.

One must not push the comparison too far though; the notorious stone is inanimate, while the Alien is an acutely sensitive organism. Its likeness to a small Nepalese beggar-child in *Kanchenjungha*, which Ray shot in Darjeeling in 1961, is much greater, says Ray. 'The Alien and the child in *Kanchenjungha* could be very close, because the child is the only one [of the characters in the film] who belongs to Darjeeling but is unaware of the fact. He's the only one who's free, who has no problems.'

That is really the essence of *The Alien*, the philosophy underlying the creature's relationship with the human beings it encounters. Ray, as ever with philosophy, chooses to leave it inarticulate. In *The Alien* it is really the humans who are alien, Ray seems to imply, because each one of them is trying to exploit his environment – an idea with ancient antecedents, perhaps especially in India, where it finds expression in the Upanishadic texts:

God is supreme and all-pervading. Enjoy by renunciation. Covet not another's wealth . . .

a Sanskrit *sloka* that made a profound impression on the saintly father of Rabindranath Tagore, the Maharshi, and later on Mahatma Gandhi. There is definitely something of Gandhi in Satyajit Ray's Alien.

Possibly that is the root cause why the ambitious project never ultimately materialized. The film was just too alien a notion for Hollywood to handle. Gandhi, after all, refused to visit the United States on the grounds that 'My well-informed friends tell me that I wouldn't even be a nine-days' wonder. After twenty-four hours I'd be relegated to the zoo.'

Ray had first visited Hollywood in 1958 at the time of *Pather Panchali*'s sensational success in the US. His closer encounter with Hollywood methods – the most bizarre experience of his career – began with a letter from Mike Wilson, a professional skin-diver, sometime film-producer and close friend of Arthur C.

THE ALIEN

Clarke in Sri Lanka, offering to raise the money in Hollywood for any science-fiction film project Ray might care to write.

From the outset Ray knew that expensive special effects available only in the West would be crucial to the film and he therefore accepted that he would also require a big name or two as a box-office draw. Otherwise he hoped to preserve virtually all the freedom he was used to enjoying in Bengal, including shooting the entire film in Bengal, with English subtitles for the sections where Bengalis were conversing.

He had in mind Peter Sellers to play Bajoria out of admiration for his roles in *Dr Strangelove* and his power of mimicry: 'the two LPs of his that I possessed held proof that he could do things with his voice and tongue which bordered on the miraculous,' Ray later wrote. Wilson was enthusiastic and within two months he and Ray were sitting down to lunch with Sellers in a vast hotel dining-room in Paris, surrounded by waiters who loved Inspector Clouseau. Although Sellers professed to admire Ray he did not know his films. At Ray's insistence *Charulata* was flown from London and screened for Sellers. Afterwards he turned to Ray red-eyed and said, 'Why do you need me? I'm not better than your actors, you know.' He gave his tentative agreement to the part though, as outlined to him by Ray.

On 1 June 1967 Ray flew to Hollywood. Wilson had cabled him that Columbia were ready to back *The Alien*, both Marlon Brando and Steve McQueen were keen to play Devlin, and that Saul Bass would mastermind the special effects, for starters. Brushing off Ray's solicitude about staying in the most chic hotel in town – 'You can't afford anything but the best, you know; you made the Apu Trilogy!' – and about the copyright line 'Mike Wilson and Satyajit Ray' on the screenplay now floating around Hollywood – 'Two heads are better than one, Maestro' – Wilson introduced Ray to the Summer of '67 in Los Angeles. The parties he went to in Hollywood mansions and the conversations he had there struck him as 'Carrollian Wonderland'. At Ravi Shankar's place he had his second encounter with Sellers who sat cross-legged after a simple Bengali dinner intently watching Shankar play. He needed to imitate the motions of playing a sitar in the film he was just then shooting, *The Party*. At Sellers's insistence Ray watched some of this shooting and found himself puzzled by Sellers's apparent inability to grasp the feebleness of his material.

123

Although Sellers assured him that he did not object to having a relatively small part in *The Alien*, Ray's instinct told him otherwise.

'I left Hollywood firmly convinced that *The Alien* was doomed,' he later wrote. It actually took a year to destroy its chances this first time round, and about fifteen years to finish it off altogether. In the meantime, apart from receiving a rave review from Sellers for *Pather Panchali*, written in verse à la William McGonagall (a favourite of Sellers since the days of the The Goons), Ray also found himself back in London with Wilson talking to Columbia UK, who had now taken over the project, and trying to avoid Wilson's suite two floors below his own at the Hilton. The one visit he did pay him there revealed a scene behind a pall of smoke

> that could have been a set-piece out of Petronius. The carpet was strewn with bodies, male and female, and Subbulakshmi [the south Indian vocalist] sang above the whirr of a movie projector and the Bengali dialogue of what turned out to be a 16mm print of my own film *Devi* flickering fitfully on a bare wall on one side of the room, a *son-et-lumière* to end all *son-et-lumières*.

It transpired that, subject to Wilson's withdrawal, Columbia was as committed as ever. But Sellers was not; in mid-1968 he wrote to Ray, explaining that he did not feel able to play the part of Bajoria as it stood. Ray, dismayed, replied in McGonagallese, referring to

> The Alien balloon
> Which I daresay will now be grounded soon.

There was no reply from Sellers.

A few months later Clarke wrote saying that Wilson had agreed to Ray going ahead on his own; he had shaved his head and gone off into the jungle to meditate (today he is known as Swami Siva Kalki). But although *The Alien* was now theoretically feasible again – and Columbia had not lost its interest in it, even without Sellers – Ray's own enthusiasm for it had cooled. He was nearing completion on another fantasy film he loved, a kind of musical about two very human characters with a magical boon, *The Adventures of Goopy and Bagha*, that would prove itself the most popular film he had ever made in Bengal. After that he planned to shoot *Days and Nights in the Forest*.

Even so, he continued to treat *The Alien* as possible, in fact through the 1970s and beyond, being variously encouraged to do so by Columbia, Peter Sellers's ex-agent, Ismail Merchant and others. Only with the appearance of *Close Encounters of the Third Kind* and more particularly *E.T.*, did Ray finally abandon his cherished project. In early 1983, following a phone call from Clarke, who had observed 'striking parallels' (in Clarke's words) between *The Alien* and *E.T.* and suggested Ray write to Spielberg pointing these out in case 'he [Ray] might be accused of plagiarism', Ray remarked casually to the Indian press that *E.T.* (a Columbia project initially), 'would not have been possible without my script of *The Alien* being available throughout America in mimeographed copies'. The *Los Angeles Times* picked up the remark and contacted personnel at Spielberg's office at Warner Brothers who apparently 'groaned' at the accusation (it was by no means the first of its kind). Spielberg himself, according to Clarke, who met him in Sri Lanka, said 'rather indignantly': 'Tell Satyajit I was a kid in high school when his script was circulating in Hollywood.'

There the matter rests. While Ray naturally regrets the demise of his project, he has no interest in pursuing the question of similarities between it and Spielberg's. What their aliens have in common, according to him, is their benign nature and the fact that each is 'small and acceptable to children and possessed of certain supernatural powers – not physical strength but other kinds of powers, particular types of vision', and that each 'takes an interest in earthly things'. But he found the alien in *E.T.* 'a bit corny at times', preferring the 'marvellous' children. Although he can understand its success he feels Spielberg's alien was less subtle than his because it was too humanized. 'Mine didn't have eyes,' he comments. 'It had sockets so the human resemblance was already destroyed to some extent. And mine was almost weightless and the gait was different: not a heavy-footed gait but more like a hopping gait. And it had a sense of humour, a sense of fun, a mischievous quality. I think mine was a whimsy.'

A.R.

Ray's 1988 sketch of the Alien.

EXT. LOTUS POND. NIGHT EFFECT
*A lotus pond in the village of Mangalpur in West Bengal. The camera
holds on a part of the surface of the pond with lotus leaves and limp
lotus stalks lit by a soft moonlight.*

*A point of light appears as a reflection in the water, grows bigger
and bigger until the pond itself is lit up. The chorus of frogs, crickets
and jackals grows in volume and is joined by a humming sound.*

*In a blaze of light something descends in the pond shattering its
placidity. A cascade of water descends on the lotus leaves, and the
camera tilts up and zooms back to a full shot of the pond.*

*A dome-like object is seen sinking into the water. The pulsating
light that emanates from it dims into total darkness as the object
slowly sinks below the surface. As the surface calms down, in the
deadly silence that now pervades, all the limp lotus stalks are seen to
straighten up and open their petals at the same time.*

Titles begin over this shot.

EXT. LOTUS POND. DAY
With the last titles, moonlight changes into the light of morning.

*A song sung casually in a boyish voice is heard – a simple, touching
folk ballad about the beauty of flowers and birdsong and fields of
grass and paddy. The camera pans to show a bamboo forest by the
pond. In that forest, a little boy is collecting twigs and singing.*

EXT. BAMBOO GROVE. DAY
This is the ten-year-old HABA, *dressed in rags, and obviously very
poor. In the bamboo grove, a bent old woman –* HABA's GRANDMA
*– is seen sweeping out dry bamboo leaves from around a shack made
out of twigs and dry coconut leaves.*

HABA *picks up a twig, straightens up, and catches sight of the
lotuses in the pond. His singing stops and his mouth falls open. Then
he turns to the old woman and shouts:*

HABA: Grandma, come and see the lotuses!

(GRANDMA *is nearly deaf.*)

GRANDMA: What?

HABA: The lotuses in the pond. Come, Grandma!

(HABA *now runs over to her and tries to drag her to the pond.*
GRANDMA *flares up.*)

GRANDMA: You know I have lumbago and you want me to come
running with you to see this and see that . . .
(HABA *has to give up. He drops the twigs and walks away.*)

EXT. TEA STALL. DAY
*The tea stall in the market place. This is where the village elders
meet in the morning and afternoon to discuss weighty problems and
to gossip.*
Sitting on hard benches in front of the shop and sipping tea are
BOSE *the advocate,* PRAMANICK *the postmaster, and* SARKAR *the
homeopath.* BOSE *turns to the homeopath.*
BOSE: Have you been to see old Narayan this morning?
SARKAR: I looked in on my way here.
BOSE: How is he?
SARKAR: Just as you'd expect him to be – at eighty-seven.
BOSE: I hope he doesn't live to see another famine. The way the
crops are looking . . .
PRAMANICK: I heard a rumble last night, and felt a chill. For a
moment I thought it was rain.
SARKAR: Same with me. I actually came out of the house to find
out.
(HABA *has arrived in the meantime and has promptly assumed
the role of a beggar. He walks up to* BOSE *with outstretched
palm.*)
HABA: Two annas for a cup of tea, please, Mister!
BOSE: So you've come pestering us again? Off with you, you
little rascal!
(BOSE *now turns to* MOHAN, *who has just arrived.* MOHAN *has
the obvious appearance of a city-bred, educated youth.*)
Good morning! How's your essay coming along?
(MOHAN *takes his seat on a bench.*)
MOHAN: What I'm writing doesn't deserve that dignified epithet,
Mr Bose. It's only a series of newspaper articles.
BOSE: Well, tell us about it. We've been watching you talking to
people and taking notes.
MOHAN: Oh, it's about village life, you know.
PRAMANICK: But what is there new to write about village life?
(HABA *is still hanging around, and now sidles up to* MOHAN.)
HABA: I'm hungry, Mister. Haven't had anything to eat since
yesterday.

PRAMANICK: And what about all the fruit you've been pinching from our orchards? 'I'm hungry,' he says!
(But MOHAN smiles indulgently at the boy.)

MOHAN: What would you like – biscuits?

HABA: And a cup of tea, Mister.
(MOHAN turns to the shopkeeper.)

MOHAN: Give this boy some tea and biscuits. I'll pay for them.
(HABA runs gleefully to the shopkeeper, while the elders on the bench scowl at him.)

BOSE: Now you've spoilt him for good. He'll make our lives miserable.
(MOHAN ignores the remark.)

MOHAN: You don't think life in the village has changed much? You may be watching television very shortly, you know.

BOSE: So we hear. But will television help to change the climate at our will? Will it bring rain when we need it? Can we ever get good crops without rain, and can people ever eat and live decently without a good harvest?

MOHAN: Well, science is trying – they are even creating rainfall artificially these days. Only on a very small scale, of course. But surely a lot is being done to improve irrigation and crops – new methods which haven't been done before.

SARKAR: Such as the tube-well that's going to come up?

MOHAN: Yes. That's a good example.

BOSE: I hear they've got a foreigner down to do the digging.

MOHAN: Yes. An American.

PRAMANICK: An American!

MOHAN: He's being employed by an Indian firm. It's a new kind of drilling machine which hasn't been used before. He's going to train up local people.
(PRAMANICK shakes his head.)

PRAMANICK: We had Americans living around here during the war. Soldiers. And I tell you, they were worse than tigers. And what they did to our women . . .
(MOHAN laughs.)

MOHAN: This is no soldier, Mr Pramanick. And I don't think this American will be around more than three or four days.
(BOSE yawns, looking up at the sky.)

BOSE: Well, the sooner he starts digging the better, because there's the sun coming out again.

EXT. SKY. DAY
There is a rent in the cloud, and the sun shines through it.

EXT. LOTUS POND. DAY
Sunlight bathes the lotus pond.

INT. CABIN OF SPACESHIP. DAY
Refracted by the pond water, sunlight enters through the round window of the spaceship submerged in the pond, and forms an undulating oval of light on the floor of the cabin. The oval forms ripples over an inert, three-fingered hand, and activates it. The hand slowly moves out of the frame.

EXT. LOTUS POND. UNDERWATER VIEW. DAY
Through the round viewport of the spaceship, we get an underwater view of the pond, consisting of fish, frogs, lotus stalks and other typical flora and fauna.
A dark form now enters the frame from below, obstructing the view. There is the head of the lone occupant of the spaceship – the ALIEN.

INT. VIEWPORT OF SPACESHIP. DAY
Now we look in from outside, and see the face of the ALIEN: *large head, sunken cheeks, small mouth, nose and ears; eyes sunken, with pupils – if they exist at all – lost in the depths of the sockets.*
The ALIEN *moves away from the window.*

INT. CABIN OF SPACESHIP. DAY
With a touch of his finger, the ALIEN *activates a control, and the spaceship begins to rise slowly.*

EXT. LOTUS POND. UNDERWATER VIEW. DAY
Looking through the viewport, we have a feeling of the spaceship slowly surfacing.

EXT. LOTUS POND. DAY
A shot of the pond surface shows the conical, spirelike top of the spaceship coming out of the water. It comes to a stop about two feet above the surface, but is still, unless one looks for it, quite effectively concealed by the lotuses.
We notice that the spaceship has the colour of gold.

INT. VIEWPORT OF SPACESHIP. DAY
The ALIEN *moves to the viewport again and looks out.*

EXT. LOTUS POND SURROUNDINGS. DAY
From the ALIEN's *point of view, we see* HABA *standing on the shore, munching a biscuit.*

INT. VIEWPORT OF SPACESHIP. DAY
Close-up of the ALIEN; *pinpoints of* green *light appear in his eye sockets and intensify. (The* ALIEN *has super-vision, and green indicates that he is observing telescopically.)*

EXT. LOTUS POND SURROUNDINGS. DAY
HABA *is thus brought up very close indeed, and we study, through the eyes of the* ALIEN, *every tiny movement of his facial muscles, his five-fingered hand, and the darting look in his eyes.*

INT. VIEWPORT OF SPACESHIP. DAY
Now the green light in the ALIEN's *eyes dims and disappears, and he moves away from the viewport.*

INT. CABIN OF SPACESHIP. DAY
The ALIEN *now activates another control which brings all the sounds of the outside world into the cabin. We hear* HABA *singing his favourite song – probably the only one he knows. We also hear bird noises, the bark of a dog, and another sound which comes, as we shall soon find out, from the drilling site.*

All these sounds make distinctive animated colour graphs on a screen on the wall of the cabin. The ALIEN *observes these patterns very carefully.*

EXT. DRILLING SITE. DAY
This is a quarter of a mile from the pond, and about twenty yards up a slope from the dirt road which connects Mangalpur to the main road a couple of miles away. A hum of activity preparatory to the commencement of the operation pervades the place now. Workers mill around, and a young bearded Sikh, obviously with some authority, goes about shouting orders.

DEVLIN, *in charge of the operation, is a brawny, brooding American in his middle thirties. He exudes an air of confidence and depend-*

ability. One feels too that he has a certain reserve of charm which he perhaps uses sparingly, and is certainly unlikely to over-use in the present circumstances of hard work in a hot, unfamiliar terrain.

Just now, DEVLIN *is holding up his lighter to* BAJORIA, *a spruce, obviously wealthy, forty-five-year-old Marwari who has engaged* DEVLIN *and his equipment for the present job.*

BAJORIA *lights his cigarette and holds it up.*

BAJORIA: You're well stocked with these, I hope.

DEVLIN: Yeah.

> (*A professional photographer,* DAS, *a thin, small man who can barely hold his Linhof steady, tries to draw* BAJORIA's *attention.*)

DAS: Sir!

> (BAJORIA *turns to the camera and smiles while continuing to talk to* DEVLIN.)

BAJORIA: I could easily get you a carton or two from Calcutta.

DEVLIN: Oh, I got enough.

> (DEVLIN *regards his lighter.*)

I'm a bit low on gas, though.

DAS: Mr Delvin!

> (DAS *wants both the men to look, and smile at the camera.* DEVLIN *obliges.*)

DEVLIN: Delvin's what I'm doin', bud. The name's Devlin!

> (DAS *clicks.*)

DAS: Thank you!

BAJORIA: I'll get you a refill. There's nothing you can't get in that city, if you have the purchasing power, ha ha!

> (DEVLIN *smiles.*)

DEVLIN: Thanks!

> (DEVLIN *turns to the workers.* BAJORIA *calls out to a stout young Marwari who has been hanging about.*)

BAJORIA: Rajni!

> (*The young man reacts, turning.*)

> (*In Hindi*) Garhisay uo dabba lana – persaadka. (*Please get the box of sweets from the car.*)

> (RAJNI *runs down to the limousine parked on the road.* DEVLIN *eyes the drilling rig.*)

DEVLIN: Well, if I don't fall off that damn thing an' break my bones or somethin' . . .

BAJORIA: (*In Hindi*) Arre Ram Ram! (*God forbid!*)

DEVLIN: . . . I reckon we'll move on to the next site tomorrow afternoon.

BAJORIA: Splendid! . . . So you feel sure about the water?

DEVLIN: (*With a quiet, casual confidence*) We'll strike water.

(DEVLIN *starts to walk slowly, his eyes on the workers;* BAJORIA *ambles alongside, gesturing to the photographer to tag along and keep shooting.*)

BAJORIA: You have no idea what this project means to me, Mr Devlin. I'm not only doing this for my own country, but also . . .

(BAJORIA *is interrupted by the young Marwari running up and handing him a round brass box.* BAJORIA *takes the box and continues to talk.*) . . . but also, I'm doing this for my own sake.

(DEVLIN *gives him a quizzical glance.* BAJORIA *smiles.*) I'm telling you because I think you'll understand. You know India is a poor country, don't you?

DEVLIN: Uh-huh.

BAJORIA: And you know I have a certain amount of wealth?

(DEVLIN *gives a sidelong glance down at* BAJORIA'*s hand holding the sweet box. All the fingers except the thumb have jewelled rings on them.*)

DEVLIN: You got some on yer fingers!

BAJORIA: What? . . . Oh, fingers – ha, ha! . . . But you know what happens to the rich man in India?

DEVLIN: Nope. What?

BAJORIA: He sticks out like a sore thumb. Because he's not a rich man in a *rich* country – not J. D. Rockefeller, but G. L. Bajoria – rich man in a *poor* country, ha ha. So he is a sore thumb, and how can a sore thumb *ever* be a popular image, Mr Devlin?

DEVLIN: I get it!

BAJORIA: So what do you think the rich man does?

DEVLIN: Takes to the bottle?

BAJORIA: No no no! He *bans* the bottle. He builds schools, parks, hospitals, temples – all for public convenience, see?

DEVLIN: And gets J. B. Devlin down to drill for water?

BAJORIA: Exactly! The best man for the job! . . . Helps the country, helps his soul, helps his image!

DEVLIN: Great!

BAJORIA: And even then he's heckled for tax returns, ha ha! (*He opens the lid of the sweet box and extends it to* DEVLIN.) Try one!

(DEVLIN *looks down at the yellow balls.*)

'Luddoos', we call them.

(DEVLIN *takes one and bites.*)

DEVLIN: Mmm . . . candy.

BAJORIA: Sanctified! (*He gestures to the photographer to take a shot of the American eating.*)

We had what we call a *puja* this morning – a sort of religious ceremony – for the success of our venture.

DEVLIN: What venture?

BAJORIA: This tube-well thing.

DEVLIN: Religious ceremony for *tube-wells*?

(BAJORIA *shrugs.*)

BAJORIA: Traditional hangover. Every venture has to be blessed by Ganesha. You know Ganesha, the elephant-headed god?

DEVLIN: Yeah. I kinda like him. He's cute.

BAJORIA: These sweets are first offered to Ganesha, then handed round to the devotees.

DEVLIN: That makes me a holy driller?

BAJORIA: Why not? Anyone who helps to bring in water here is doing holy work.

(DEVLIN'*s attention has strayed to a group of young Santhal girls across the road.*)

DEVLIN: Say, y' got some holy chicks out there.

BAJORIA: What? (*He follows* DEVLIN'*s gaze and sees the girls.*)

Oh, chicks – ha ha, I like that! Is that the latest term for women?

(DEVLIN *eyes the girls with dreamy approbation.*)

DEVLIN: Yeah . . . but it's still the same women!

(*The girls have started to walk now, arm in arm, and they are a picture of vivacity and animal grace.* BAJORIA *seems disconcerted by* DEVLIN'*s absorption. Is he a womanizer? Is he going to bring the project a bad name?*)

BAJORIA: Tribals . . . sort of Untouchables.

DEVLIN: Uh-huh.

BAJORIA: All married, of course. Marry early. Very early. And . . . er . . . great hunters.

DEVLIN: Hunters?

BAJORIA: The menfolk. The males. They – er, come in both sexes.

DEVLIN: Uh-huh.

BAJORIA: I've seen them bring down rabbits at a hundred yards. Bow and arrow, you know.

(*One of the girls has now spotted* DEVLIN, *and points him out to the others. They start giggling, and nudging one another.*)

DEVLIN: Hey, they're cute, aren't they?

(BAJORIA *nods wisely.*)

BAJORIA: Yeah . . . but I shouldn't start getting ideas, my dear fellow. I should – ahem! – confine all drilling, if you know what I mean, to the – er – virgin soil.

(DEVLIN *grins.*)

After all, you'll be through in a week, at the most.

DEVLIN: And then y' gonna hand me that key to your harem, eh?

(BAJORIA *raises his eyes heavenwards.*)

BAJORIA: Arre Ram Ram!

DEVLIN: No harem?

BAJORIA: At least, I can assure you that the city of Calcutta is not lacking in chicks.

(DEVLIN *grins broadly. He is obviously developing an affection for the Marwari.*)

DEVLIN: What's your first name, Badge?

BAJORIA: Gaganlal. G–A–G–A–N–L–A–L.

DEVLIN: H'm. Mind if I call you Gag?

(BAJORIA *winces.*)

BAJORIA: No no no, not Gag, *please* – Gug.

DEVLIN: Gug?

BAJORIA: Gug. Shorten it, but don't strangle it.

DEVLIN: OK, Gug!

(BAJORIA *looks at his wrist watch.*)

BAJORIA: Well, I think I'll buzz off now. If there's anything more I can do for you . . .

DEVLIN: Tell Ganesha to turn the heat down a bit.

BAJORIA: Oh certainly, certainly! . . . Best of luck, and have a good dig!

DEVLIN: See you tomorrow.

(DEVLIN *strides off toward the rig and* BAJORIA *toward his limousine.*

    MOHAN *has been hovering in the vicinity, and now scurries after* BAJORIA.)

MOHAN: Excuse me –

    (BAJORIA *stops and turns.* MOHAN *draws up before him.*)

I'm from the Calcutta Herald.

BAJORIA: What?

MOHAN: Calcutta Herald. The daily paper.

BAJORIA: Yes?

MOHAN: I'd like to do a little piece on this drilling rig.

BAJORIA: Well, the best man is Mr Devlin there. It's his baby. If you don't pester him too much . . .

MOHAN: Oh no!

    (MOHAN *turns to go.* BAJORIA *stops at the door of the car and turns to* MOHAN *again.*)

BAJORIA: I say –

    (MOHAN *stops and looks back.*)

Come here a moment.

    (MOHAN *walks back.*)

This paper – is it Left or Right?

    (MOHAN *hesitates.*)

MOHAN: It's – er . . .

BAJORIA: Never mind. Are you in favour of this project or not?

MOHAN: Oh, I think it's a very good project.

BAJORIA: Good. You know my name?

MOHAN: Mr Bajoria.

BAJORIA: Initials?

MOHAN: G. L., I think?

BAJORIA: G. L. . . . Good.

    (BAJORIA *gets into his car along with* RAJNI *and the photographer.*

    HABA *has arrived in the meantime and has assumed his professional stance, his hand stretched out before* DEVLIN.)

HABA: Baksheesh, Sahib, baksheesh!

DEVLIN: You get me a green coconut and I'll give you baksheesh.

    (MOHAN *arrives just in time to translate for* DEVLIN.)

MOHAN: (*In Bengali*) Saheber janya daab perhe ditay parbi akta?

(*Could you fetch the Sahib a green coconut?*)

    (HABA *gives a quick nod and darts off.*

DEVLIN *is about to walk off when* MOHAN *accosts him.*)
Mr Devlin!

DEVLIN: Yeah?

MOHAN: I'm a reporter, and Mr Bajoria just asked me to see
you. Could you tell me very briefly about this new drilling
rig?

DEVLIN: Digs deeper wider quicker – OK?

MOHAN: And do you think . . .

DEVLIN: Some other time, Charlie – gotta spud in now . . .
sorry.

(DEVLIN *turns to go.* MOHAN *notices something and reacts
sharply.*)

MOHAN: Oh, Mr Devlin!

(DEVLIN *stops and turns, plainly irritated.*)

DEVLIN: Now what?

MOHAN: Just a moment . . .

(MOHAN *walks up behind* DEVLIN, *crouches down and lifts a
hairy caterpillar off the seat of his trousers with the aid of his
pencil. He holds the insect up for* DEVLIN *to see.*)
They're poisonous.

DEVLIN: Hey, we got slugs like them back home.

(MOHAN *smiles.*)

MOHAN: So can I say you don't feel like a stranger here?

(DEVLIN *starts to peel off his shirt.*)

DEVLIN: You kiddin'? Say, it's a regular home from home!

(DEVLIN *walks off.* MOHAN *drops the caterpillar on the ground
and squashes it with his sandal.*)

EXT. COCONUT GROVE. DAY

HABA *climbs dexterously down a coconut tree, picks up the fruit he
has dropped from above, and is about to make off for the drilling site
when shouts are heard:*

VOICE: (*Off-screen*) Thief! Little scoundrel!

(HABA *takes to his heels. A man –* KUNDU, *the owner of the
tree – picks up a stone and throws it at the boy. The stone hits*
HABA *squarely on the back of his head and makes him stumble
forward.*

MOHAN, *on his way back from the drilling site, sees* HABA's
predicament and runs up to the boy. HABA *gets up on his feet,*

rubbing the back of his head with his free hand. The hand gets smeared with blood.

 The KUNDU *comes charging up from behind.* HABA *flees.* KUNDU *looks accusingly at* MOHAN.)

KUNDU: Why did you let the boy go?

MOHAN: Was that your coconut?

KUNDU: Yes! – And I'm going to turn that boy over to the cops one of these days.

 (MOHAN *brings out his purse.*)

MOHAN: How much did the coconut cost?

 (KUNDU *simmers down.*)

KUNDU: It's not that. You don't have to pay. But you musn't encourage that boy. He is a born thief.

EXT. DRILLING SITE. DAY

HABA *comes charging up the slope.*

HABA: Salaam, Sahib, salaam!

 (DEVLIN *walks over.*)

DEVLIN: Thanks.

 (DEVLIN *hands the boy a shining eight-anna bit and collects the coconut.*)

 OK?

HABA: OK!

 (HABA *runs off.* SINGH, *the young bearded Sikh, walks over.*)

SINGH: Shall I cut it for you, Chief?

INT. VIEWPORT OF SPACESHIP. DAY

The ALIEN *is still looking out.*

EXT. LOTUS POND SURROUNDINGS. DAY

From the ALIEN's *point of view, we see* HABA *come back from the drilling site. He flicks the coin up in the air and catches it as it drops. Then he feels his wound again. It is still bleeding.*

INT. VIEWPORT OF SPACESHIP. DAY

The ALIEN's *eyes turn green.*

EXT. LOTUS POND SURROUNDINGS. DAY

The ALIEN *sees the blood in close-up. Then he sees the wound when* HABA *bends over to wash his hand in the pond.*

INT. VIEWPORT OF SPACESHIP. DAY
The green light in the ALIEN's *eyes dims. He appears thoughtful as he hangs his head down slowly. Then he reacts sharply as a new thumping sound suddenly invades the cabin of the spaceship.*

INT. CABIN OF SPACESHIP. DAY
A new, bold sound pattern, low in the scale and sharply rhythmic, forms on the screen.

EXT. DRILLING SITE. DAY
The drill has started to operate, and its ponderous rhythmic thud now fills the countryside.

Fade out.

Fade in:

INT. NARAYAN'S BEDROOM. NIGHT
Evening in NARAYAN's *bedroom. Eighty-seven-year-old* NARAYAN, *the oldest inhabitant of Mangalpur, lies seriously ill.* SARKAR, *the homeopath, is feeling his pulse. Gathered round his bed are members of* NARAYAN's *family: his grandson* KESHAB *and his wife and their two children. We also see* BOSE, PRAMANICK *and* MOHAN *near the door.*
SARKAR finishes his examination and gets up. He walks toward the door, turning to the grandson.
SARKAR: He might last through this night, but tomorrow being a full moon . . .

EXT. NARAYAN'S HOUSE. NIGHT
The doctor and the visitors come out of the house. BOSE *turns to* MOHAN.
BOSE: You may make a note of this for your essay, Mr Mohan: You and I are certainly not likely to live to such ripe old age – because we just don't have the stamina. We may have wiped out malaria, and we may have injections and vaccinations and all the rest of them, but we just can't compete with our forefathers. They lived in a golden age, Mr Mohan – science or no science – because they ate more

wholesome food. No adulteration . . . everything clean and
pure . . . milk one anna per seer . . . can you imagine?
(MOHAN *smiles.*)
MOHAN: I'll certainly make a note of that, Mr Bose. Thanks!

EXT. DRILLING SITE. NIGHT
DEVLIN *comes out of his tent. Soft moonlight bathes the gaunt form
of the drilling rig. A breeze is blowing. A chorus of jackals rends the
stillness of the night air.* DEVLIN *draws in a deep breath, surveying
the strange, unfamiliar, undulating rural landscape. He takes his
whisky flask from his hip pocket and drinks. The words of a ballad
form on his lips, and he hums.*

*Now he reacts to a sound of drumming. Tribal drums of the
Santhals. It comes from a village diagonally across the paddy-fields.
After a moment's thought,* DEVLIN *starts to walk in that direction.*

EXT. BO TREE BY THE TEMPLE. NIGHT
*He has to go past the Bo tree beside the Kali Temple. Below the tree
sits a Sadhu with beard and matted hair, his body smeared with ash.
Beside him are seated his two disciples, one of whom is preparing a
chillum of ganja.*

DEVLIN *slows down to take a better look, then resumes his normal
gait.*

EXT. KALI TEMPLE. NIGHT
DEVLIN *walks past the temple now. A ceremony is in progress and
we hear the beat of gongs and cymbals. Two women come out of the
temple and walk up in the direction of* DEVLIN. *At the sight of him,
they stop, turn around and scamper off, drawing their saris across
their faces.* DEVLIN *gives a half-amused, half-puzzled shrug, then
continues to walk, humming the ballad in snatches.*

INT. MOHAN'S BEDROOM. NIGHT
MOHAN *is glancing through the day's newspaper before getting down
to resuming his article. His newly married wife,* KALYANI, *comes in
plaiting her hair. A girl of about nineteen,* KALYANI *has a soft,
gentle beauty, although the observant will sense the intensity that
hovers below the surface.*

*She stands with her back to the window, looking down at her
husband hunched over the paper spread open on the bed. After a*

moment's silence, KALYANI *speaks; and she could just as well be
speaking to herself.*

KALYANI: I wish you were doing a series on the mountains.
Then we could go up to Darjeeling. That would be a real
honeymoon.

(MOHAN *keeps looking at the paper.*)

MOHAN: Did you see a moving light in the sky last night?

KALYANI: What moving light?

MOHAN: They say some observers in Karachi, Kathmandu, and
some parts of West Bengal have seen a moving light.

(KALYANI *keeps looking down at* MOHAN, *who turns a page.*
KALYANI *sighs.*)

KALYANI: Does anything ever move here, really? Does anything
ever happen? I wonder . . .

(MOHAN *folds up the paper.*)

MOHAN: Strange!

KALYANI: What's strange!

MOHAN: You and I sitting and talking here in this sleepy hole –

KALYANI: *You* were not talking – *I* was talking.

MOHAN: All right, you talking and I reading the paper in this
sleepy hole, while *they* are getting ready to land the first men
on the moon. Can you imagine what that means, Kalyani?

(KALYANI *moves up near the bed behind* MOHAN *and runs her
fingers down his neck.*)

KALYANI: I know what it doesn't mean. It doesn't mean better
prospects for you, because they won't send you to the moon
to report on the landing!

(MOHAN *gets up and starts pacing the floor with excitement.*)

MOHAN: But just think – for the first time in the history of
mankind – which means the first time in a million years –
man will set foot on the moon!

(MOHAN *has moved up to the window, and is looking up at the
moon.* KALYANI *comes to his side and looks up.*)

KALYANI: Will they find the old woman at the spinning wheel,
I wonder?

MOHAN: I'm afraid she'll be where she's always been – in our
nursery rhymes.

KALYANI: But they won't be the same anymore – the nursery
rhymes. Uncle Moon! How could Uncle Moon ever be the

same with those Americans trampling all over him? It makes me so sad . . .

(MOHAN *laughs and puts his arms around* KALYANI.)

MOHAN: *Shunya!* . . . It means space and it means zero – isn't that wonderful?

(KALYANI *leans back, warm and contented in her husband's embrace.*)

You know who discovered the zero?

KALYANI: Discovered the what?

MOHAN: Zero.

KALYANI: What are you talking about?

MOHAN: One-two-three-four-five-six-seven-eight-nine – zero! You put a zero after one and it becomes one more than nine. Every zero added multiplies it ten times. Isn't that wonderful? Well, *we* discovered that zero – an unknown Indian – way back in the time of the Upanishads . . . And that changed the course of history, by changing the course of mathematics. But then – then we lost ground.

(MOHAN *moves away from the window and starts pacing the floor.* KALYANI *keeps looking at her husband.*)

KALYANI: But this is not your essay, is it?

MOHAN: It's all linked up, Kalyani. It's all part of a chain – a process. What we were, what we might have been, and what we have become . . .

KALYANI: Then it's going to take a long time to write, isn't it?

(MOHAN *takes the hint at last. He smiles at* KALYANI, *and there is a hint of apology in the smile.*)

MOHAN: Not so long, Kalyani, and you can help to shorten it.

(KALYANI *is surprised.*)

KALYANI: Me? How?

(MOHAN *becomes serious.*)

MOHAN: I'll tell you how. You know I've been talking to the men, sort of interviewing them? Well, I want you to talk to the women. There are certain things which only the women can tell you. This business of family planning, for instance. I want to know how they feel about it. You could ask them if they're using –

(KALYANI *quickly claps her hand over* MOHAN's *mouth.*)

KALYANI: That's enough!

(MOHAN *manages to free his mouth to speak.*)

MOHAN: Why, what's the matter?

KALYANI: I'm sorry to disappoint you, but I'm not the shameless modern sophisticate that you thought you'd married.

(MOHAN *smiles and pulls* KALYANI *toward him for a warm embrace.*)

MOHAN: Thank God for that!

EXT. SANTHAL VILLAGE. NIGHT

The tribal dance has reached a peak of frenzy. The girls, about twenty in number, have interlocked their arms and have formed a semicircle. They step backwards and forwards to the music in a rhythmic, undulating movement. The men play the drums and the flutes.

DEVLIN *sits on a mound a little way away, drinking the local wine from a clay pot. His feet keep tapping to the beat of the music.*

The girls are oblivious of their surroundings, dancing, singing, laughing, their silver ornaments glinting in the moonlight.

DEVLIN *finishes the drink and throws the pot away. Then he gets up and saunters up close to the dancers. He walks round behind the girls, appraising them with a true connoisseur's eye. Unerringly, he selects the prettiest girl, and takes a position behind her so that she almost touches him at the end of each backwards movement.*

DEVLIN *stands watching the movements of the girl's body – the bare shoulders glistening in the moonlight, the nape of the neck, the way the plaited hair has been knotted into a bun, and the way flowers and ornaments have been stuck into it. He puts out his hand and deftly pulls out a silver ornament from the girl's hair. The girl doesn't notice it.* DEVLIN *twirls the ornament in his fingers for a few moments, then pushes it back into place as the girl gets close again. Next he pulls out a flower which he doesn't bother to replace. Holding it up to his nose, he moves up to watch the drummers, then puts the flower over his ear, Tahitian-style, and saunters away.*

INT. REVEREND'S BEDROOM. NIGHT

The grey-haired Reverend, BISWAS, *lives in a cottage by the side of his modest little church. He is now busy fixing the mosquito curtain in his bedroom. His eyes go to the little window, and he reacts, then goes out of the room in something of a hurry.*

EXT. CHURCH. NIGHT

BISWAS *comes out of his cottage and walks up to the wicket.* DEVLIN *stands outside, cigarette in mouth, clicking away at his lighter which doesn't seem to work.* BISWAS *greets the American.*

BISWAS: Good evening!

(DEVLIN *looks up at* BISWAS *and nods.*)

DEVLIN: Evening . . . You have a light? I've run out a gas!

(BISWAS *is flustered.*)

BISWAS: Light? Light?

(*He runs back into his cottage and comes out with a lighted candle, guarding the flame carefully with his free hand.* DEVLIN *lights his cigarette.*)

DEVLIN: Thanks. This your church?

(BISWAS *nods, smiling.* DEVLIN *walks in through the wicket and takes a few steps toward the church.*)

Who comes to pray?

BISWAS: I have my little . . . flock – the Santhals.

DEVLIN: Who?

(BISWAS *points in the direction of the music.*)

BISWAS: Santhals. The tribals.

(DEVLIN *is surprised.*)

DEVLIN: They Christians?

BISWAS: Some of them. You see, they are the aboriginals of the country. They had no conception of God as we know Him.

DEVLIN: You converted them?

(BISWAS *shrugs.*)

BISWAS: There were others before me, too. It is not an easy task . . .

(DEVLIN *glances in the direction of the music.* BISWAS *is embarrassed.*)

Those that come to church, they sing hymns. Not like this.

DEVLIN: You don't like this kinda music?

(BISWAS *doesn't know what to say. He suspects the American likes the music. There is a moment's awkward silence. Then* DEVLIN *smiles at* BISWAS.)

Well, thanks for the light.

(DEVLIN *walks away.* BISWAS *looks on, holding the candle in his hand. The words of a ballad come floating to him, making a strange counterpoint to the tribal music.*)

DEVLIN: (*Off-screen*) 'If you're travellin' in the north country far

144

Where the wind hits heavy on the borderline
Remember me to one who lives there . . .
She was once a true love of mine . . .'

INT. CABIN OF SPACESHIP. NIGHT
In the cabin of the spaceship, the ALIEN *is still studying the sound patterns formed on the screen. The components now are the shrilling of crickets, croaking of frogs, and the distant boom of the Santhal drums. To these a new element is now added –* DEVLIN's *song.*
DEVLIN: (*Off-screen*) 'I'm wonderin' if she remembers me at all
Many times I've hoped and prayed
In the darkness of my night
In the brightness of my days . . .'
(DEVLIN's *voice fades out.*
The ALIEN *moves his hand and activates another control.*)

EXT. LOTUS POND. NIGHT
The spaceship in the pond. Its top opens like a lid.
Through the opening, the ALIEN *comes out, a cross between a gnome and a famished refugee child: large head, spindly limbs, a lean torso. Is it male or female or neuter? We don't know. What its form basically conveys is a kind of ethereal innocence, and it is difficult to associate either great evil or great power with it; yet a feeling of eeriness is there because of the resemblance to a sickly human child.*
The ALIEN *stands poised on the top of the spaceship for a few seconds. Then he takes a leap, and lands gently, almost weightlessly, on a lotus leaf. He looks down on the surface of the water, gets down on his knees, touches the water with his finger.*
Blue lights now appear in his eye sockets, enabling the water to be examined microscopically.

MICRO-DETAIL OF WATER
Germs, amoeba and other minute earthly forms of life are revealed to the ALIEN. *He can even listen to the sound they make while they swim.*

EXT. LOTUS POND. NIGHT
Now the lights in his eyes dim, and the ALIEN *stands up. There is a certain tension about him, as if he has to be watchful of traps; then*

suddenly, in a series of fantastically quick, short steps over the lotus leaves, the ALIEN *reaches the shore of the pond. He looks down at the grass, examines a blade, and is off hopping into the bamboo grove.*

EXT. BAMBOO GROVE. NIGHT
There the ALIEN *sees a small plant. His eyes light up with a yellow light. He passes his hand over the plant, and flowers come out. A thin, soft, high-pitched laugh shows the* ALIEN *is pleased. He plucks a flower, puts it into his mouth, and hops on all fours to an ant-hill.*

He pokes the ant-hill with his fingers, and causes agitated ants to swarm out of their holes. The ALIEN's *eyes turn blue.*

MICRO-DETAIL OF ANTS
The ALIEN *observes the ants microscopically, and attunes his ears to make audible the sounds made by the insects.*

EXT. BAMBOO GROVE. NIGHT
Looking up, the ALIEN *laughs to see a swarm of fireflies dancing round a mango tree. He leaps up, catches hold of a mango branch and keeps swinging, while the fireflies dance around him.*

Poised in mid-air, the ALIEN *sees* HABA's *shack. He goes flitting through the air to reach the door of the shack. He peers inside.*

INT. HABA'S SHACK. NIGHT
The ALIEN *sees* HABA *huddled in sleep on a mat. The* ALIEN's *eyes now turn a glowing red. This enables him to see* HABA's *respiratory system, and to listen to his regular heartbeats.*

The red in the ALIEN's *eyes now turn violet, enabling him to look into* HABA's *brain, and sink into his subconscious.*

HABA'S DREAM
HABA *is dreaming, and the* ALIEN *becomes part of his dream. We see* HABA *and the* ALIEN *happy, playing hide-and-seek in a strange black and white world of geometrical forms.*

INT. HABA'S SHACK. NIGHT
The light in the ALIEN's *eyes now dims, and with another high-pitched laugh, he is gone from the bamboo grove.*

EXT. PADDY-FIELD. NIGHT EFFECT
The ALIEN *now arrives at the paddy-field. The wide open spaces
seem to delight him, and he dances around for a while – then he
notices the withering crop and examines a paddy plant. His eyes turn
yellow, and he goes whirling about in the field while all the paddy
around him ripens and stands aspiring in the moonlight.*

Standing on the tip of a ripe paddy plant, the ALIEN *looks up at
the sky.*

NIGHT SKY WITH MOON
He sees the nearly full moon in the sky, and seems fascinated by it.

EXT. PADDY-FIELD. NIGHT
The ALIEN *turns on his telescopic green eye-lights.*

NIGHT SKY WITH MOON
*The moon is brought up close for inspection, so that its gigantic orb
marked with craters and mountains and valleys now fills a good half
of the sky. Inspection over, the* ALIEN *pushes the moon back in place.*

EXT. PADDY-FIELD. NIGHT
The ALIEN *now jumps off the plant, and flits back laughing to the
spaceship.*

EXT. GOVINDA'S HUT. DAY (NEXT MORNING)
GOVINDA, *the peasant, comes out of his hut, rubbing his eyes and
yawning. He pats his cattle, yawns again, and ambles towards his
field.*

EXT. GOVINDA'S PADDY-FIELD. DAY
The sight that meets GOVINDA'S *eyes makes his mouth fall open. A
slow-witted man,* GOVINDA *can only scratch his head, walk over to
examine the ripe paddy, walk back again, shake his head, and scratch
it again.*

EXT. GOVINDA'S PADDY-FIELD. DAY
*The news of the miraculous paddy has spread, and the whole village
has gathered at the field to see the strange sight. A group of young*
PEASANTS *have clustered round* GOVINDA, *and are pestering him
with questions.*

FIRST PEASANT: Tell us how it happened, Uncle Govinda. Tell us how you did it.

SECOND PEASANT: There should be no secrets between us, Uncle Govinda. Tell us what you put in the soil.

THIRD PEASANT: I saw that sahib walking past your field last night. Did he do something? Did you bribe him to do it?

(But GOVINDA *can only shake his head in utter bewilderment.)*

GOVINDA: I swear to God I know nothing about it. I'm as innocent as you are.

(BHATTACHARJI, *the temple priest, is also among those present. He suddenly makes a ringing declaration.)*

BHATTACHARJI: This is indeed a miracle. All praise to Mother Annapurna!

(A murmur rises from the crowd. Some people make obeisance to the paddy, but BOSE *is still sceptical.)*

BOSE: You know, we shouldn't discount the possibility of that American having done something with some new fertilizer or other. Since Panchu says he's actually seen him around here . . .

(BHATTACHARJI *glowers at* BOSE.)

BHATTACHARJI: I'm shocked at what you say, Bose. If man knew how to ripen paddy overnight, then there would be no need for God to exist, and the world would be rid of all its ills – which, as you know, is still not the case.

(The sentiment is echoed by others, and BOSE *has to yield.*

MOHAN *is among those present. He looks tense, having smelled a story. He takes the still-bemused* GOVINDA *aside.)*

MOHAN: How do you feel about what has happened, Govinda?

GOVINDA: How do I feel? I ask you, Babu, how *you* would feel if you had a one-year-old child – a sickly child, to be sure, but whom you gave all your love and care, and suddenly one morning you found him a full-grown man. How would you feel then, Babu?

(MOHAN *takes rapid notes in his pad, but is distracted by* HABA's *shouting.)*

HABA: Come and see the new temple, the new temple!

(BOSE *turns round.)*

BOSE: What new temple?

HABA: The new temple in the lotus pond . . . and the lotuses are all in bloom!

(HABA *has already started to run in the direction of the lotus
pond, and the crowd turns to follow the beggar boy.*)

INT. CABIN OF SPACESHIP. DAY
*A babble of human voices invades the cabin, and makes new patterns
on the screen. The* ALIEN *applies his eyes to the viewport.*

EXT. POND SURROUNDINGS. DAY
The crowd arrives, led by HABA, *who points triumphantly to the
spaceship in the pond.*
HABA: There it is!
   (*There are expressions of amazement from the crowd.*)
BOSE: Wonderful!
PRAMANICK: And look at the colour – a golden temple!
   (*But* HABA *has some further information to give.*)
HABA: My friend is in there. He is the one who has caused all
   the fruits and the flowers to grow.
   (*He is promptly knuckled on the head by* BOSE *for saying so.*)
BOSE: 'My friend is in there' – indeed! Don't you start showing
   off again, you little rascal!
   (PRAMANICK *agrees with* BOSE.)
PRAMANICK: This is a religious matter, and talking like that will
   incur the wrath of the deity.
   (*A somewhat deflated* HABA *recedes into the background.*
   MOHAN *has been intrigued by* HABA's *story. He now goes up to
   the boy and draws him aside.*)
MOHAN: What friend have you got in there, Haba?
HABA: It's a little boy like me, Babu. He came down from the
   stars.
MOHAN: Indeed? And how did you know that?
HABA: He told me. He was in my dream last night.
   (MOHAN *realizes the boy is not all there.*)
MOHAN: Oh, I see. Very good.
HABA: And he's healed my wound, too.
   (HABA *rubs the back of his head. The wound has obviously
   healed. But* MOHAN's *attention has strayed to the thing in the
   pond. He keeps looking at it with a puzzled expression, while
   the men around him talk about it.* BOSE *has turned to* BHATTA-
   CHARJI, *the priest, who looks thoughtful and hasn't spoken so
   far.*)

BOSE: Well, Bhattacharji, what have you got to say?

(BHATTACHARJI *slowly shakes his head.*)

BHATTACHARJI: I was thinking of . . . something . . . it said in the almanac.

BOSE: What did it say?

BHATTACHARJI: About a visitation . . . in this part of the world . . . about this time of the year . . .

BOSE: What kind of a visitation?

BHATTACHARJI: A powerful entity . . .

BOSE: A benevolent entity?

BHATTACHARJI: I can't remember. I'll have to look it up again . . .

(*At this point, somewhat unexpectedly,* MOHAN *picks up a stone and throws it at the spaceship. It produces a sharp metallic clang on contact. The elders in the crowd turn menacingly towards him.*)

BOSE: That was a very foolish thing to do, young man.

(MOHAN *manages to keep his composure.*)

MOHAN: I was only trying to see if it was metal. It could have been a stage prop, you know – made of pith or wood or something.

BHATTACHARJI: Do you realize that you risked sacrilege by doing that?

(MOHAN *steps back from the shore and withdraws into the shade of a tree.*

A part of the crowd has already moved to the other side of the pond. On that side is the mango tree on the edge of the bamboo grove. The owner of the tree is a man named KUNDU, *whom we have already met as the owner of the coconut tree, who stoned* HABA.

There is a stampede towards the tree, which has come out with fruit – a very unusual thing to happen in October. KUNDU *now plants himself in front of the tree, facing the crowd, and declares his ownership in no uncertain terms.*)

KUNDU: This tree belongs to me. The fruits belong to me. They are gifts from the Mother Goddess. Remember, anybody who steals them commits a sacrilege.

(BOSE *suddenly leaves the shore of the pond and runs off.*)

EXT. BOSE'S COURTYARD. DAY

BOSE *comes whizzing in through the door of the courtyard and runs straight up to a guava tree and looks anxiously up at the branches. His wife calls out from the kitchen.*

MRS BOSE: What's the matter? Why are you looking up at the tree?

    (BOSE's *face darkens.*)

 OSE: This is a gross injustice.

EXT. DRILLING SITE. DAY

At the drilling site, where digging is in progress, a man from Mangalpur runs up the slope and whispers the news of the miracle to one of the workers.

    The news begins to spread. DEVLIN, *climbing down from the rig, notices the buzz of conversation.*

DEVLIN: OK, break it up . . . what's going on here?

    (*One man had moved away from his position.* DEVLIN *glowers at him.*)

    Where the hell d'ya think y're goin'? Get back on the job!

    (*The man meekly resumes his position.* SINGH *draws up beside* DEVLIN, *who stands cleaning the grease from his hand with a piece of waste.*)

SINGH: A very strange thing has happened, chief. A temple has –

DEVLIN: Aw, get outa here!

    (DEVLIN *walks away to meet* BAJORIA, *who had watched the sudden explosion of temper and had been waiting for a lull to greet the American.* BAJORIA *puts out his hand, smiling.*)

BAJORIA: Good morning, Jim! . . . You don't mind my calling you Jim?

DEVLIN: Nope! 'Cept my parents called me Joe.

    (DEVLIN *brings out his packet of Luckies.*)

BAJORIA: Oh, sorry, I thought the J stood for –

DEVLIN: OK. How're you this morning?

BAJORIA: Fine! (*He lights* DEVLIN's *cigarette and hands him the lighter.*)

    It was easier to get a gas lighter than just gas.

    (DEVLIN *is surprised and touched.*)

DEVLIN: Oh! – Say, thanks!

BAJORIA: A pleasure. How's it going?

DEVLIN: Great. See the water?

BAJORIA: So your hunch paid off?

DEVLIN: Usually does. On schedule. Stay for lunch?

BAJORIA: I'll stick around a bit – if it's not inconvenient.

DEVLIN: No – 's all right . . . I'll be right back.

>(DEVLIN *strides off to attend to some unfinished business.*
> BAJORIA *calls* SINGH, *who comes over quickly.*)

BAJORIA: What was the trouble, Singh?

SINGH: No trouble, sir. Just something which has happened in that village over there. They say a temple has come out of a pond . . .

BAJORIA: A temple?

SINGH: Yes, sir.

BAJORIA: Out of a pond? What do you mean – out of a pond? Through the water?

SINGH: That's what they say, sir.

>(BAJORIA *looks thoughtfully in the direction of Mangalpur.*)

EXT. LOTUS POND SURROUNDINGS. DAY

KALYANI *looks around for her husband. She spots him in the shade of a clump of bamboos and walks over.* MOHAN *looks up at* KALYANI, *who is obviously piqued.*

KALYANI: You might at least have come home and told me.

MOHAN: Sit down, Kalyani.

>(*We see a group of women clustered on the opposite bank. Some are making obeisance. Some throw flowers into the water. The conversation is hushed, and there is already an air of religious awe pervading the place.*
> KALYANI *sits down beside her husband.* MOHAN's *pad and pencil lie on the grass beside him.*)

KALYANI: I thought I'd find you happy and working, and now I find you worried and –

MOHAN: It's upset all my calculations, Kalyani.

>(KALYANI *keeps silent. She is already familiar with her husband's moods.*)
> When it first happened, I thought, my god, what a story! But now . . .

KALYANI: Now what?

>(MOHAN *sighs.*)

MOHAN: You know, I don't think I could ever make a good reporter. A reporter mustn't think for himself. He should

just set down what he sees and what he hears. He should
be a conveyor belt, no more. But *I* can't help thinking. I
can't help asking why such a thing should happen in the
twentieth century, and I can't find an answer. How can I
write? It's the answer I want to write about, and I can't find
it.
(The sound of a car breaks the spell, and both KALYANI *and*
MOHAN *rise to their feet.*
BAJORIA'*s limousine arrives in a cloud of dust and pulls up by
the lotus pond.* MOHAN *rises, his eyes narrowing. He ignores*
KALYANI.*)*
KALYANI: Lunch is ready, and Uncle Romesh is waiting.
MOHAN: You two eat lunch, please. I'll come when I've finished
my work here.
*(*MOHAN *gets up and takes a few steps towards the car.* KALYANI
looks on for a while, then goes away.
BAJORIA *has come out of the car, and stands gazing at the
glistening gold of the spaceship.)*
BAJORIA: My god!

INT. CABIN OF SPACESHIP. DAY
Inside the spaceship, the ALIEN *keeps his eyes glued to the viewport,
observing* BAJORIA *and the limousine.*

EXT. LOTUS POND SURROUNDINGS. DAY
BAJORIA *has spotted* MOHAN *and nods a friendly greeting.* MOHAN
moves up.
BAJORIA: There must be a good story for you there.
*(*BAJORIA *indicates the spaceship.* MOHAN *smiles.)*
You belong here?
MOHAN: No. Calcutta.
BAJORIA: What is this village called?
MOHAN: Mangalpur.
BAJORIA: Ah, the Land of Well-being! . . . A good name.
*(*BAJORIA *turns to the crowd, who have been watching him with
great curiosity.)*
(In Bengali) Apnader gramer naam khub bhalo achche –
khub bhalo! *(Your village has got a beautiful name.)*
(He rubs his hands in satisfaction and turns to MOHAN *again.)*

Well, ever seen a temple like that before?

MOHAN: Never.

BAJORIA: Must be the only one of its kind in existence. I've made quite a study of them. You know I have been restoring ruined temples all over India?

MOHAN: I do, Mr Bajoria.

BAJORIA: Are you in favour of such restoration or not? Give me a frank answer. I won't put you in gaol if you say no.

(MOHAN *smiles.*)

MOHAN: Then I must say no, Mr Bajoria.

BAJORIA: Then you must give me your reason.

MOHAN: I feel works of art should be left alone.

BAJORIA: Even crumbling-down ones, eh? Even when they are also places of worship? What happens in fifty years' time, then? No works of art and no places of worship – ha, ha . . . Don't you see? At least I'm giving religion a new lease of life!

MOHAN: I'm sure you have God Himself on your side, Mr Bajoria.

BAJORIA: I'm sure I do. I really believe I do. That temple there tells me so. It was God's own design that it should come out so near my drilling site.

MOHAN: And how do you think it got there in the first place?

BAJORIA: Very simple. It has always been there, below the pond. Maybe below the soil. It's the explosives they used over there that's pushed the thing up to the surface. Simple.

(MOHAN *makes no further comment.* BAJORIA *starts to rub his hands and to hum.*)

INT. VIEWPORT OF SPACESHIP. DAY

The green *light in the* ALIEN's *eyes now slowly turns* red.

X-RAY OF BAJORIA

BAJORIA – *from the* ALIEN's *point of view – has turned into an animated X-ray photograph.* BAJORIA *stops singing and speaks.*

BAJORIA: I haven't the slightest doubt that Mangalpur is going to turn into the greatest place of pilgrimage in India, very soon.

EXT. LOTUS POND SURROUNDINGS. DAY

A shrill unearthly laughter greets this announcement. BAJORIA *stops dead with one foot in the car and turns round.*

BAJORIA: Who was that?

> (*The people look at one another, puzzled. Even* MOHAN *is puzzled.*)

Silly fools!

> (BAJORIA *gets into the car. Then he beckons to* MOHAN *who walks over.* BAJORIA *lowers his voice when he speaks to* MOHAN.)

You want to make good? Make a mark as a reporter?

MOHAN: Naturally!

BAJORIA: Then don't do any rash reporting on this. Don't write your story yet, understand? Wait till tomorrow and I'll give you an exclusive story that'll make the headlines in every paper you can think of – Left, Right, Front, Back or Middle – understand?

MOHAN: Thank you . . .

> (*But* BAJORIA *has already wound up his window.*)

EXT. DRILLING SITE. DAY

DEVLIN *comes out of his tent with a towel. He seems in a good mood and is humming. He calls out to his assistant.*

DEVLIN: Singh!

> (SINGH *runs up.* DEVLIN *washes his face and hands.*)

Pull it down. We'll eat lunch now. Tell the crew they can go an' have a look at that pagoda.

SINGH: I want to go too, chief!

DEVLIN: OK but back at two o'clock sharp.

SINGH: OK, chief!

> (BAJORIA *has arrived in the mean time, and has walked up the slope toward* DEVLIN.)

BAJORIA: An auspicious day, it seems.

> (DEVLIN *wipes his face and hands with the towel.*)

DEVLIN: Come an' have a cold beer.

> (*He walks towards the air-conditioned trailer,* BAJORIA *following.*)

INT. TRAILER. DAY

The two men enter. BAJORIA *hums as he sits down.*

BAJORIA: (*Humming*) Nananana nahnana nah nah nah
      Nanahna nah nana nah nah nah . . .

   (DEVLIN *rummages in the ice box for the drinks.*)

DEVLIN: You sing?

BAJORIA: Only when I'm very happy. Or very sad. This is a
   bhajan – a devotional song.

   (DEVLIN *gets out the beer and pours it out.*)

   You keep time by clapping when you sing. (BAJORIA *demonstrates, singing and clapping*)

         Raghupati Raghava Raja Ram
         Patiatapavana Sita Ram
         . . . like this!

   (DEVLIN *claps in applause, then indicates the beer. They clink glasses and drink.*)

   (BAJORIA *licks his lips before speaking.*) Mr Devlin, I have a
   proposition.

   (DEVLIN *takes a sidelong glance at* BAJORIA *as he puts his feet up on the table.*)

DEVLIN: Proposition?

   (BAJORIA *nods.*)

BAJORIA: You see, there's a pond in that village out there, and
   in that pond there's a temple. Its top is sticking out of the
   water.

DEVLIN: Uh-huh.

BAJORIA: I want that pumped out. The water, I mean.

   (*There is a pause before* DEVLIN *speaks.*)

DEVLIN: Why?

BAJORIA: Well, *if* it's a temple – and it's very likely to be one,
   because its coming out has coincided with all sorts of extraordinary supernatural –

   (DEVLIN *interrupts.*)

DEVLIN: You believe in all that crap?

BAJORIA: There's no other explanation, Joe. These things don't
   happen without good reason.

DEVLIN: But that's crazy!

   (BAJORIA *leans forward.*)

BAJORIA: There are more crazy things happening in this blessed
   country, Joe, than are dreamt of in *your* philosophy!

DEVLIN: Philosophy's got nothin' to do with it, Charlie; I'm a driller. You get me out here all the way from Butte, Montana, to bring in water, and now you're talkin' of temples and extraordinary ponds an' supernat– . . . oh boy!

(DEVLIN *drinks, shaking his head.* BAJORIA *keeps smiling.*)

BAJORIA: What's wrong with that, Joe? Didn't you know business and religion make the most wonderful cocktail in the world, eh? Didn't you?

(DEVLIN *regards* BAJORIA *with a new interest, not unmixed with a certain admiration.* BAJORIA *is drumming on the table with his fingers. His diamond rings flash and catch* DEVLIN's *eye.*)

DEVLIN: Goldfinger, eh? . . . Well, can't say you done too badly if that's how you done it.

(BAJORIA *pushes the unfinished glass aside and leans forward even more.*)

BAJORIA: That's how I done it, yes, *but* – what I done so far is nothing, Charlie, noth-thing. But what I gonna do now is something. I want you to help me, Joe.

DEVLIN: Me?

BAJORIA: Yes, my dear fellow, you. I want you to *pump* that water out, so that I can cover the floor of that pond with marble, and build marble steps leading down from all four sides, and arches, and pillars, and a little marble plaque to say: Salvaged and restored by Gaganlal Laxmikant Bajoria! . . . That village out there, Joe, is going to be the holiest place in India.

DEVLIN: Yeah, but what I don't get is – why pick on me? All you need is a salvage pump –

BAJORIA: I'll *get* the salvage pump.

DEVLIN: OK – and get an Indian to do the dredging job, while we move on to the next drilling site. You got fine workers here. You don't need me!

(*The confident, mysterious, playful smile doesn't leave* BAJORIA's *face. He lowers his voice almost to a whisper.*)

BAJORIA: I do!

DEVLIN: No, you don't.

BAJORIA: Yes I do, Mister Joe, or I wouldn't have come to you. I'm *not* a man of whims. I'm a very level-headed, logical-minded man, and my every action is very carefully planned *and* executed – *with* a purpose.

(BAJORIA *pauses for effect.* DEVLIN *pulls the sandwich box towards him and takes out a sandwich.*)

DEVLIN: I'm listening.

(DEVLIN *pushes the sandwich box towards* BAJORIA *who ignores it.*)

BAJORIA: Do you have a gun?

(DEVLIN *stiffens.*)

DEVLIN: What d'you need a *gun* for?

BAJORIA: *I* don't need it, arre baapre! – you do.

DEVLIN: Now hold on just a minute – you want a shooter, get yourself another boy – I don't want trouble.

BAJORIA: Do you *have* a gun?

DEVLIN: Yeah – and it's gonna stay right where it is.

(BAJORIA *smiles and shakes his head, as if he is up against a stubborn child.*)

BAJORIA: What trouble do you anticipate, Joe, and from whom? You think I don't pull any weight in this country? And what makes you think you'll have to *use* the gun? All I want is that you should have it with you. Just in case.

DEVLIN: In case o' what?

(BAJORIA *leans forward.*)

BAJORIA: I'll tell you. Now, you have this pond, and you have this temple in the pond. (*He shifts his beer-glass to the middle of the table to lend visual support to his description.*) OK?

DEVLIN: Yeah.

BAJORIA: Yeah. A very holy temple. Now, I, Gaganlal Bajoria, want the water pumped out because I want a real, solid temple where people can walk in and worship. In fact, my motive is perfectly religious. But suppose – just suppose – the villagers get it into their heads that I'm after that gold.

(DEVLIN *frowns.*)

DEVLIN: What gold?

BAJORIA: Oh, sorry – forgot to tell you – the temple is covered with gold.

DEVLIN: No kiddin'?

BAJORIA: No kidding at all. I'm ninety-five per cent certain it is gold. But the thing is – they may have the *same* suspicion.

(DEVLIN *nods his head slowly.*)

DEVLIN: H'm . . .

BAJORIA: You see?

DEVLIN: Yeah. So you want me with a gun so they don't string you up on that mango tree, is that it?

(BAJORIA *gets excited.*)

BAJORIA: But, Joe – you know how riots start here? You know how the Indian Mutiny started? Out of nothing – noth-thing! . . . The moment they smell a rat they'll go for their hammers and sickles – and what then? Before you can say Rajagopalacharia, I'm a dead man.

DEVLIN: Yeah . . .

(DEVLIN *brings his feet down from the table.*)

BAJORIA: A dead man, Joe! A bloody corpse!

(DEVLIN *gets up.*)

DEVLIN: Saint Bajoria.

BAJORIA: But, Joe –

DEVLIN: You know, I have a good mind to grab the next plane back home and to hell with the drilling.

(BAJORIA *throws up his arms.*)

BAJORIA: Arre arre – this is terrible, Joe. I don't know why you take this attitude, really. This is no crime I'm asking you to do. *They* pump the water out – the Indians do it. You just stand by with the gun – buss! Nothing more. This is no crime! After all, even the US President makes you do things you don't *like* to do!

DEVLIN: Yeah, and we vote him out of office.

(DEVLIN *gets back to his chair, picks up another sandwich.*)

BAJORIA: You're not going to vote me out for this, Joe. I'm not asking you to do this for nothing.

(DEVLIN *looks at* BAJORIA *with a sharpened interest.* BAJORIA *smiles.*)

You have a family, Joe?

(DEVLIN *slowly shakes his head, keeping his eyes fixed on* BAJORIA, *trying to anticipate his next move.*)

A girl friend? A 'chick'?

DEVLIN: What's the gimmick?

(BAJORIA *laughs shortly, puts his hand in his inside pocket and brings out his cheque book.*)

BAJORIA: I don't know what that word means, Joe – but I want you to give her a little Exmuss gift, from me. A little ahead

of time, but then you won't be here for Exmuss. (*He puts
the cheque-book down on the table, opens it and flattens it.*) You
have nothing to lose, Joe. And I'm sure it doesn't bother
you that you might arouse the wrath of an unknown Hindu
deity – possibly with four arms and fourteen legs?
(BAJORIA *now brings out his fountain pen from the same pocket.
It's a gold Parker.*) And if you are worried about your image,
let me tell you – Americans are widely known to indulge in
a lot of strange activities, right here in India, just for the
heck of it . . . far stranger than pumping water out of a
pond, Joe!
(BAJORIA *is about to write out the cheque, but is thwarted by*
DEVLIN *casually taking the pen out of his fingers.*

BAJORIA *looks up, surprised.* DEVLIN *speaks at last.*)

DEVLIN: Ever get bit by a coyote?

BAJORIA: Coyo – . . .?

DEVLIN: I once knew a guy who had a coyote bite him when he
was a kid. He had the same kinda . . . same kinda . . .
(DEVLIN *draws labyrinth patterns in the air with the pen to
indicate the kind of mind* BAJORIA *has got.*)

EXT. GOVINDA'S PADDY-FIELD. NIGHT
*It is night, and a full moon has risen over the paddy-field. The wail
of jackals is heard from the Santhal village across the field.*

INT. NARAYAN'S BEDROOM. NIGHT
Moonlight comes in through the barred window of NARAYAN'S *bedroom and falls on the dying man's face.* NARAYAN *is in a state of
coma. There are six or seven people in the room, all looking on silently
and waiting for the end.*

Suddenly the people in the room react, leaning forward. NARAYAN
has opened his eyes. His eyeballs turn to the window.

EXT. NIGHT SKY
We see the starry sky from NARAYAN'S *point of view.*

INT. NARAYAN'S BEDROOM. NIGHT
Now NARAYAN *lifts his emaciated right hand. With great effort, he
straightens his forefinger and points to the sky. His lips began to work
in the effort to form a word. His grandson bends over him.*

KESHAB: Do you wish to say something, Grandpa?
(NARAYAN's *voice seems to come from a great distance.*)
NARAYAN: A . . . Ava . . . Avatar!
(*The hand drops down.* NARAYAN *is dead.*)

EXT. CHURCH SPIRE. NIGHT
The cross over the church in the Santhal village is seen against the full moon.

INT. CHURCH. NIGHT
The Reverend, BISWAS, *is holding a special service for his small congregation. The sermon, of which we hear the concluding words, relates to the miracles.*
BISWAS: (*in Bengali*) . . . These are but revelations of the Lord's presence, of His powers, His pity. He who makes the laws of nature has it in His power to break them too. And that is how miracles occur, and such miracles are an aspect of His love – for us, His children. The benefit we gain is in the knowledge we gain. And the more we know Him, the more we love Him, and the more we love Him, the more we remember Him in our prayers . . .

EXT. TEMPLE SPIRE. NIGHT
The symbol of the spire on the Hindu temple is seen against the full moon.

INT. TEMPLE. NIGHT
BHATTACHARJI, *the priest, is conducting a religious ceremony in the temple to the beat of gongs and cymbals and the blowing of conch shells.*

EXT. SPACESHIP. NIGHT
The spire of the spaceship is seen against the full moon.

INT. CABIN OF SPACESHIP. NIGHT
Inside the spaceship, the ALIEN *is looking intently through the view-port, using his telescopic vision.*

EXT. BAMBOO GROVE. NIGHT

From the ALIEN's *point of view,* HABA *is seen prowling about in the bamboo grove. We see him catching a frog and putting it into his sack. Then he moves on stealthily and approaches a group of fireflies.*

EXT. SANTHAL VILLAGE. NIGHT

DEVLIN *walks into the square in the Santhal village, where the dancers had been the previous night. It puzzles him to see that tonight the place is deserted. Even the huts around seem to be empty. A lone pariah dog barks out at him. He walks around aimlessly for a while, then goes off towards the church.*

EXT. SANTHAL CHURCH. NIGHT

BISWAS *is pacing about in the moonlight outside his cottage. He sees* DEVLIN *and reacts.*

BISWAS: Good evening.

    (DEVLIN *nods.*)

DEVLIN: Hi, Reverend! Feels kinda spooky tonight. Where's everybody?

    (BISWAS *smiles.*)

BISWAS: You mean the dancers? They've gone to a fair ten miles away, in another village.

DEVLIN: H'm.

    (BISWAS *seems tense, as if he wants to say something but doesn't quite know how to begin.*)

BISWAS: Er – Mister . . .

DEVLIN: Devlin's the name.

BISWAS: Mr Devlin . . . you're American, aren't you?

DEVLIN: Yeah.

BISWAS: An engineer?

DEVLIN: Yeah.

BISWAS: Do you mind if I ask you a question?

    (DEVLIN *smiles.*)

DEVLIN: 'Pends on the question!

BISWAS: What do you think of the miracles?

    (DEVLIN *replies after a brief pause.*)

DEVLIN: I don't think.

BISWAS: Don't think what?

DEVLIN: Don't think. Period.

    (DEVLIN *brings out his whisky flask.*)

BISWAS: Do you believe science is the answer to everything?
DEVLIN: No more 'n this!
   (DEVLIN *holds up the flask to* BISWAS.)
   Care for a drink?
   (BISWAS *smiles and shakes his head.*)
BISWAS: I've spent seventeen years trying to cure my congregation of the habit.
   (DEVLIN *drinks.*)
DEVLIN: If you can't lick 'em, join 'em.
BISWAS: (*Puzzled*) Pardon?
   (DEVLIN *doesn't bother to elucidate.*)
DEVLIN: I'd figured on getting one of those drums to take back with me.
BISWAS: A Santhal drum?
DEVLIN: Yeah. Great drums.
BISWAS: I'll arrange to send you one.
DEVLIN: Kind of you . . . What's that?
   (*From the village of Mangalpur across the paddy-fields comes the sound of a funeral chorus.*)
BISWAS: Somebody died. They're carrying the dead body to the burning ghat.

EXT. LOTUS POND SURROUNDINGS. NIGHT
NARAYAN's *bier, carried on the shoulders of six persons, with three or four others following in the rear, moves past the pond.*

INT. VIEWPORT OF SPACESHIP. NIGHT
The ALIEN's *head appears, looking out.* Green *eye-lights appear in the eye sockets.*

EXT. LOTUS POND SURROUNDINGS. NIGHT
In big close-up, the ALIEN *sees the upturned profile of the dead* NARAYAN *lying on the bier.*

EXT. BURNING GHAT. NIGHT
DEVLIN *walks past the burning* ghat *and sees the body of* NARAYAN *arriving. Slowing down for a second,* DEVLIN *then resumes his normal gait.*

163

EXT. THE BO TREE. NIGHT
DEVLIN *now reaches the Bo tree where the Sadhu sits with his two
disciples. The* chillum *is being passed round.*

DEVLIN *stops to look, then steps forward. The Sadhu turns a
reddening but not unfriendly eye toward him.*

DEVLIN *settles himself on top of an uneven block of stone, the
remnant of an old pillar. For a few seconds he looks on at the old
mendicant, then speaks.*

DEVLIN: You a Sadoo?
(*The Sadhu smiles and moves his head in the faintest suggestion
of a nod.* DEVLIN *smiles too.*)
What's that mean? (*pause*) I mean . . . like what's it all
about, man?
(*The Sadhu takes the* chillum *from one of his disciples, and
drags deeply.* DEVLIN *looks on appreciatively. Then he extends
his whisky flask towards the Sadhu.*)
Wanna trade vices? This is good liquor. (*The Sadhu takes
the flask.* DEVLIN *keeps his hand stretched out for the* chillum,
*which comes only after the Sadhu has downed the liquor in one
mighty gulp.* DEVLIN *takes the* chillum, *but has trouble with
the grip.*) Hey, how d'you hold this damn thing? (*One of the
disciples demonstrates.*)
Aha!
(*This time* DEVLIN *gets it right. He applies his mouth to the
opening and pulls.*)

EXT. BURNING GHAT. NIGHT
NARAYAN's *dead body has been placed on the funeral pyre.* KESHAB,
NARAYAN's *grandson, places a log of wood on the corpse for the
cremation. More logs of wood are placed by other men.*

From behind an akanda bush, the ALIEN *watches. His eyes turn
red.*

INSIDE NARAYAN
We see NARAYAN's *respiratory system: no movement, no heartbeat.*

EXT. BURNING GHAT. NIGHT
The ALIEN's *eyes turn from red to an intense white.*

INSIDE NARAYAN
This time there is a return of movement.
  The first heartbeat is heard, then a second.

EXT. BURNING GHAT. NIGHT
KESHAB *leans over the dead body to place a log on it across the chest.*
But on the face of the corpse the eyelids move slowly apart, and the
lips part.

  KESHAB *reacts, drops the log, and starts shaking. A hoarse scream*
comes out of his mouth.
KESHAB: My god! He's alive!
    (KESHAB *bolts.*
      There is general panic as others react, scream and bolt.
    SARKAR, *the homeopath, walks up to the corpse.*
      The ALIEN's *eyes dim.*
    SARKAR *looks down at the corpse.* NARAYAN *is as dead as ever.*
      Behind the akanda bush, the ALIEN *laughs mischievously and*
    skips away.)

EXT. BO TREE. NIGHT
DEVLIN *has had a few pulls at the* chillum *and is beginning to feel*
its effect. His eyes are reddening too. He turns them to the Sadhu.
DEVLIN: Wise guy, eh?
    (*The Sadhu begins to shimmer a little in his field of vision as*
    DEVLIN *looks around. Everything within his field of vision seems*
    to shimmer.) Jesus!
    (DEVLIN *looks at the* chillum *in his hand, then, with a swift*
    movement, throws it away. We hear the crack as it contacts a
    hard surface. Almost immediately, the Sadhu does likewise with
    the flask, flinging it in the same direction as the chillum. DEVLIN
    is caught unawares, but reacts strongly and is up on his feet.)
    Hey, what the . . .
    (*He retrieves the flask which had landed just alongside the broken*
    chillum. *He glowers at the Sadhu, who remains mute and*
    inscrutable.) OK – I get it! (*He walks back and sits down*
    again, breathing hard and keeping his eyes on the Sadhu.)
    Y'know the rope trick?
    (*There is no answer from the Sadhu.*) Y' gotta bed o'nails
    aroun' here somewhere?
    (*Still no answer.*)

I bet ya don't. (DEVLIN *sniggers*.) I bet ya sleep on a mattress.
Yeah! You're no better'n Joe Devlin . . . maybe not so good!
(DEVLIN *looks hard at the Sadhu, as if he is looking for chinks
in his armour.*) Yeah, maybe not so good. I bet ya can't dig
a hole 'n' strike water – can ya? . . . Ya' seen the water? Ya
seen it pukin' up out there? Ya seen the rig that's done it?
It's a helluva rig, Sadoo . . . an' it's gonna do somethin' fer
this goddam country . . . Ya done somethin' fer this country? . . . Nah! Ya been all worked up sittin' an' doin' nothin'
– yeah! A helluva lot ya done . . .
(DEVLIN *gets up on his feet and walks a few steps. He holds
on to a low-hanging branch of the Bo tree and looks up at the
sky. The full moon has rings around it.* DEVLIN *turns to the
Sadhu, pointing his finger up at the moon.*) See that thing up
there? Ya wanna go sit there an' smoke pot? (DEVLIN *laughs
as the image forms in his mind.*) 'Hindoo Sadoo Gets Nirvana
on Moon' – how d'ya like that, eh? Ya can buy real estate
there soon – yeah! Yanks're gonna land there an' no kiddin'
. . . 'n' the Reds too – land on that goddam stinkin' satellite
. . . An' it takes a lotta guts to do that, an' a lotta dough,
Sadoo. Ya gotta be up on yer feet an' moving' – ya gotta be
on the *go* – like *me*, see? Ya gotta *live*. Y'r not livin', y'r
dead. Ya got no problems – the dead've got no problems
. . . (DEVLIN *points to the flames in the funeral pyre in the
distance.*) That roastin' stiff out there got no problems . . .
no income tax . . . no draft . . . no broads . . . no busted
drainpipes . . . no – no –
(*He stops as he notices the Sadhu's stare. There is something
unnervingly intense about the stare.*)
Hey . . . you a fish or somethin'? . . . I ain't seen ya blinkin'
yet . . . Don't ya blink?
(*The Sadhu keeps on staring unblinkingly.* DEVLIN *starts to
fidget. He can't take his eyes away from the Sadhu's face.*)
Wha'ya keep starin' at me for? . . . Ya think I'm wrong?
(*Now the Sadhu shimmers a little more, but his red eyes keep
staring out remorselessly at the American.*)
Maybe ya got problems too . . . yeah! Maybe you licked
'em all, so now ya can sit an' . . . sit an' . . .
(*A jackal suddenly cries out from a bamboo thicket near by.*

166

DEVLIN *starts. Then he picks up a piece of stone and hurls it savagely into the depths of the thicket.* Stop yellin', y' – !
The momentum of the throw somehow gives DEVLIN *the strength to wrench himself away from the Sadhu's hypnotic stare, and he staggers away towards the drilling site.)*

EXT. BAMBOO GROVE. NIGHT
To go to the drilling site DEVLIN *has to walk through the bamboo grove.*

    The grove is now like the inside of some strange Gothic church, the bamboos arching and intersecting overhead, the moonlight filtering in through the mesh of leaves, and dappling the ground covered with dry leaves and undergrowth. Wild flowers, yellow, white and blue, shimmer where they catch the moonlight. The shadows are lit by swirling constellations of glow-worms, adding to the unearthly atmosphere which makes even DEVLIN *pause and look around. Is he alone, or is there someone else in the grove keeping an eye on him?*

    DEVLIN *shouts to make sure.*

DEVLIN: Hey!
    (There is an echo, but in a shrill high-pitched voice. DEVLIN *sniggers, and continues to walk.*
    Suddenly, in a clearing, DEVLIN *is face to face with the* ALIEN.
    DEVLIN *stops dead and stares at the childlike form. He leans forward to get a better look. The* ALIEN, *poised on the thin branch of flowering plant, stares back at* DEVLIN.)
    That you, kid? . . . Nah . . . we ain't met before, have we?
    (The ALIEN *looks on with his green eye-lights.)* What kinda peepers y' got?
    (The ALIEN's *eyes dim, but he keeps looking on.)*
    Wha'y'all keep starin' at me for? Ain't seen a Yank before? Go on home. Beat it.
ALIEN: Beat it!
DEVLIN: Aw, shucks! *(He turns round and continues to walk. The* ALIEN *hops after him soundlessly.* DEVLIN *senses he's being followed, stops, and turns. The* ALIEN *stops, too.)*
    You want money? Baksheesh? Here. *(*DEVLIN *tosses an eight-anna bit to the* ALIEN *and walks away. The* ALIEN *picks up the coin and laughs happily.)*

INT. MOHAN'S BEDROOM. NIGHT

MOHAN *stands at the window, looking out pensively. Somewhere a clock strikes midnight. Outside,* KALYANI's *voice is heard.*

KALYANI: It's midnight.

    (MOHAN *turns.* KALYANI *stands by the bed, then slowly sits down on the edge of the bed, and hangs her head down.*)

MOHAN: What is it, Kalyani?

KALYANI: Nothing.

    (MOHAN *notices the slight tremor in her voice, moves up, puts his hand below her chin and lifts her head up. There are tears in* KALYANI's *eyes.* MOHAN *sits down by her side.* KALYANI *lets her head droop and rest on her husband's shoulder.*)

MOHAN: It's only that I – I want things to fall into place and they refuse to, Kalyani.

KALYANI: It's because you let your mind wander too much. You think of the moon and the stars and the zero and . . . and . . . don't think of me at all!

    (MOHAN *puts his arms around her.*)

MOHAN: It's not thinking, Kalyani, it's worrying. I'm worrying about something I can't fathom. I'm worrying about a mystery. You're no mystery to me, Kalyani.

KALYANI: I wish I were – if only to be a little more in your thoughts.

MOHAN: But you *are* in my thoughts, now!

KALYANI: And what are those thoughts – may I know?

    (MOHAN *smiles.*)

MOHAN: They are thoughts which tell me not to think, but to –

    (MOHAN *makes* KALYANI *lie down and kisses her warmly. Then he keeps his face very close to hers and keeps looking into her eyes.*)

KALYANI: But you're thinking again.

MOHAN: I'm not thinking. I'm looking. I'm looking into a pond.

KALYANI: A lotus pond?

MOHAN: No, but it's shaped like a lotus petal. It's fringed by dark foliage, and there's a mysterious temple in the middle which is shaped like a . . . like a zero, and there's a very mischievous deity in it who takes a man's mind off his work, and who sparkles like a –

    (MOHAN *suddenly stops.*)

KALYANI: Like a what?

MOHAN: Star . . . Haba said something about a star . . .

KALYANI: And now you have to think of Haba.

(MOHAN *is tense.*)

MOHAN: But you don't realize, Kalyani – sometimes a child has more wisdom than an –

(MOHAN *suddenly sits up, his eyes shining with excitement.*) Where's that paper?

KALYANI: What paper?

MOHAN: When did we read about the moving light? – Yesterday! . . . That means the light was seen two nights ago, and the temple –

(MOHAN *springs out of bed and rushes out of the room barefooted. Kalyani sits about with an annoyed pout, her hair falling loose about her shoulders.*)

EXT. MOHAN'S HOUSE. NIGHT

MOHAN *comes running out of the house on to the street, and is pulled up by the unexpected spectacle of a group of people marching up in his direction.*

BOSE'S *voice is heard.*

BOSE: (*Off-screen*) There's Mr Mohan . . . Lucky we don't have to wake him up.

(*The group arrives, and we find it consists of* BOSE, PRAMANICK, BHATTACHARJI, *Narayan's grandson* KESHAB, *the peasant* GOVINDA, *and a few others.* BOSE *is the spokesman.*) We're going into town to report to the authorities tomorrow morning, Mr Mohan. There's some kind of witchcraft going on here.

MOHAN: You mean, the thing in the pond? You don't think it's a temple?

(BOSE *turns to* BHATTACHARJI.)

BOSE: You tell him, Bhattacharji.

BHATTACHARJI: I looked up the almanac. There's nothing in it about the emergence of a new temple, but it is clearly stated that some untoward events will occur about this time of the year, caused by the juxtaposition of Saturn and Mercury.

BOSE: These miracles are not for our good, Mr Mohan. At least, they're not for the general good. Do you think a benevolent deity should be a partial deity, benevolent only to certain chance individuals, some of whom are not even decent people? We have nothing against Govinda here – but he refuses to harvest his crop, and most of the other peasants have turned against him! And Keshab here swears that he saw his grandfather open his eyes on the funeral pyre.

(KESHAB *gets excited.*)

KESHAB: Yes, I did! No matter what you say, I saw him open his eyes, and the doctor had pronounced him dead.

(SARKAR *gets flustered.*)

SARKAR: But you were all there when he died – you saw the spasm – and the heart had stopped beating. I'll swear to it to the end of my life.

BOSE: But what makes us most sceptical about a benevolent deity is Kundu's mango tree. You know, Mr Mohan, he is the meanest man in the village – the meanest, the stingiest and the most unscrupulous. He has done nothing in his whole life to deserve the blessings of any deity.

(MOHAN *at last has a chance to speak.*)

MOHAN: Mr Bose, I'm glad you don't believe that the thing in the pond is a temple with a deity in it, but I would still urge you not to do anything in a hurry – at least, not tomorrow morning.

BOSE: Why not, Mr Mohan?

MOHAN: Well, first of all, you must admit that there's no proof that the thing in the pond is actually out to do harm. It hasn't really done anything *directly* harmful – like spreading a new epidemic, for instance. It has only done things which man would like to do with the help of science, but hasn't succeeded in doing. But since it is obviously something powerful, we should be careful not to antagonize it. We should proceed very cautiously.

BOSE: What is your theory, Mr Mohan, and how do you propose to tackle the thing in the pond?

(MOHAN *hesitates.*)

MOHAN: Well, I think it has some connection with some other planet – but not astrological – not as the almanac says.

(*The elders do not react favourably to this.*)

BHATTACHARJI: So you propose to write your own almanac?

MOHAN: No, no – but, you see, planets are not just influences; they are also – not all of them, but some – habitable worlds, like ours, and – and . . .

(MOHAN *suddenly realizes it is useless to try to elaborate on his spaceship theory to the assembled crowd and there is an awkward silence as he trails off.*)

BOSE: Well, however that may be, we are now concerned not with other planets, but with this little village of ours. For us, this is our world, our planet. Whatever your theories may be, and whatever you may wish to do about the thing in the pond, I hope you won't team up with the Marwari and the American.   .

MOHAN: Why do you say that, Mr Bose?

BOSE: Because they both seem up to no good. I think the Marwari plans to go for that gold. We could tell that from the way he was looking at it this afternoon. And the American . . . well, he turns out to be no better than we expected; he went to the Santhal village last night.

MOHAN: I promise to see, as far as I can, that no harm comes to the village; but you must cooperate by not doing anything in a hurry. You must give me a little time.

BOSE: All right. We give you twenty-four hours. After that, we take things into our own hands.

(*The crowd disperses.*)

EXT. LOTUS POND SURROUNDINGS. NIGHT

MOHAN *comes running and stops by the pond, tense and trembling with excitement. The top of the spaceship glistens in the moonlight, and a gentle breeze sways the lotuses.* MOHAN *looks up at the sky and down again at the capsule. A crackly voice is suddenly heard wailing from the bamboo grove. It is the voice of* HABA'S GRANDMA.

GRANDMA: Haba, where are you, Haba? Where's the little devil gone this time?

(MOHAN *turns around and sees the old woman standing outside her shack, looking around helplessly.* MOHAN *runs up to her.*)

EXT. BAMBOO GROVE. NIGHT

MOHAN *comes running up to the old woman.*

MOHAN: Where's Haba gone? I heard him singing only a little while ago.

(GRANDMA *shakes her head.*)

GRANDMA: Oh, he's such a pest, he is. He was sitting by the

pond and singing, and I asked him to come to bed, and he said . . . he said . . . oh, I don't know what he said.

MOHAN: Please try to remember what he said. It's very important.

GRANDMA: I'm an old woman. I can't remember . . . He said . . . he said . . . he had a new home, he said . . . or something like that. I don't remember . . .

(MOHAN *paces about restlessly, unable to decide what to do. Now* DEVLIN *can be heard, singing his favourite ballad, from the drilling site across the grove.*)

DEVLIN: (*Off-screen*)

If you're travellin' in the north country far

Where the wind hits heavy on the borderline . . .

(MOHAN *dashes off toward the drilling site.*)

EXT. DRILLING SITE. NIGHT

MOHAN *rushes up the slope, panting.* DEVLIN *sits slumped in his chair outside his tent, his legs stretched out, singing to the accompaniment of a guitar.*

DEVLIN: 'Remember me to one who lives there

She was once a true love of mine . . .'

(MOHAN *moves up toward* DEVLIN.)

MOHAN: Mr Devlin!

(DEVLIN *stops singing and looks up with some displeasure and considerable surprise at* MOHAN.)

I'm sorry for coming like this, but there's something I must tell you.

(DEVLIN *recognizes* MOHAN.)

DEVLIN: You the guy from the newspaper?

MOHAN: Yes . . . er . . . You must have heard about the thing in the lotus pond, Mr Devlin.

(DEVLIN *stops strumming and turns to* MOHAN.)

DEVLIN: Look, if y've come to talk some more about the temple, y'can go back, 'cos I've had my bellyful.

MOHAN: But that thing is *not* a temple, Mr Devlin, it's a spaceship.

(DEVLIN *screws up his face.*)

DEVLIN: WHAT?

MOHAN: It's a spaceship.

DEVLIN: How d'ya spell it?

(MOHAN *knows that* DEVLIN'S *being sarcastic.*)

MOHAN: It's a spaceship, Mr Devlin. A spaceship from some other planet. There was a story in the papers yesterday about a moving light seen in the sky over some parts of India. I think that light was a spaceship, and that spaceship has landed in that pond. And I . . . think it has someone in it with super-powers, and I think he has caused the miracles to happen.

(DEVLIN *speaks after a pause.*)

DEVLIN: You get paid to think like that?

MOHAN: No, but –

DEVLIN: Then why d'ya think like that? Why don't ya go home to bed an' sleep?

(DEVLIN *takes up his guitar again and starts to play, but* MOHAN *is adamant.*)

MOHAN: But I'm convinced, Mr Devlin. It's not just a suspicion, it's a certainty. Everything falls into place if you believe it's a spaceship, and from a planet which is far more advanced than ours.

(DEVLIN *stops playing and looks* MOHAN *squarely in the face.*)

DEVLIN: OK, so it's a spaceship from Pluto – so what?

MOHAN: In that case, we should do something about it. We should make contact with whoever is in it. We should try to make friends with him. Don't you see, we could learn things from him.

DEVLIN: Whaddya mean *we*? Listen, why doncha go home 'n' write about it? We'll talk to him or her or it when we pump out that water tomorrow mornin' . . .

'If you go when snowflakes storm,
When rivers freeze . . .'

(MOHAN *has suddenly gone pale.*)

MOHAN: The water in the pond?

DEVLIN: 'And summer ends . . .' Yeah, so you don' have to swim to church . . .

'Please see she has a coat so warm
To keep her from the howlin' wind . . .

MOHAN: *You* are pumping the water out? It's *your* idea?

(DEVLIN *stops singing, but keeps up the guitar.*)

DEVLIN: Say, ya got a kid livin' aroun' here that goes about in his birthday suit?

173

(MOHAN *is in a daze, and* DEVLIN's *question doesn't register on him.*)

    'Please see if her hair hangs low.'

This one's got no hair . . . and three fingers . . . must be a leper or somethin' . . .

    'It rolls and flows all down her breast

    Please see for me if her hair's hangin' low . . .'

(MOHAN *muses.*)

MOHAN: If that thing is not a temple but a spaceship, and if you start pumping the water out . . .

(DEVLIN *loses his temper at last.*)

DEVLIN: Look, lemme ask you a simple question – why in hell's name would a spaceship from Mars or Venus or Jupiter or any other goddam planet or solar system land *here*? *If* they're intelligent, why *here*? They're not Joe Devlin. They got no drillin' job to do for Bajoria!

MOHAN: But why must they come with a purpose, Mr Devlin? I think they came here because their ship just happened to land here and not anywhere else.

DEVLIN: I know why they came here – they came for the pot, an' it's made 'em a bunch of Sadoos!

(DEVLIN *starts up the guitar again.* MOHAN *gets up and turns to go.*)

    'I'm wonderin' if she remembers me at all,

    Many times I've hoped and prayed

    In the darkness of my night

    In the brightness of my days . . .'

EXT. LOTUS POND SURROUNDINGS. DAY

It is early morning of the next day. A pale, limpid light bathes the lotus pond. Some of the older men and women of the village – particularly those who don't share the doubts of BOSE *et al. – have gathered on the shore of the pond to pay homage to the unknown new deity. They make obeisance to the 'temple', fill up their brass pots with the water of the pond and throw flowers in it.*

    BAJORIA's *limousine, bumping up the village path, shatters the calm and causes the women on the shore to cover their heads with their saris. The limousine pulls up, and a truck carrying the salvage pump lumbers up and pulls up behind it.*

Now the whole village turns up at the pond, drawn by the sound of the vehicles.

BAJORIA, DEVLIN, *the photographer* DAS *and* RAJNI *get out of the car.* BAJORIA *is dressed Indian-fashion, in a dhoti and a long coat buttoned up to the neck.* DEVLIN *has brought his weapon – a light machine-gun – which draws gasps and comments from the crowd. He carries it in a very professional manner, and there is an extra magazine taped to the one fitted. He walks over to the edge of the pond to have a look.*

MOHAN, *unshaven, stands a little away from the crowd with* KALYANI *by his side. He casts a grim look in the direction of* BAJORIA, *who ignores him.* BAJORIA *now advances toward the crowd, and walks past it with folded palms and a benign smile on his face. The crowd greets him with an uncomprehending stare. Anxious, but still smiling, he sidles up to* DEVLIN, *who still has his eyes fixed on the spaceship.*

BAJORIA: Great, isn't it?

(DEVLIN *doesn't answer.*)

Shall we start pumping? I think we ought to start pumping, Joe. Delay might be – er, fatal.

DEVLIN: You know, Gug . . .

BAJORIA: I know, Joe. I know we mustn't delay. We mustn't give them time to think. They're not in a very good mood, Joe.

DEVLIN: That looks a damn sight too queer to be a temple –

BAJORIA: Nonsense. All temples are queer, Joe. You don't know how queer they are. This one's the least queer of them all.

DEVLIN: – and a damn sight too clean to be an old one.

BAJORIA: It's washed by the water, Joe. Like fish. Fish are clean! Ever caught a dirty fish? For God's sake get on with the pumpkin . . . pumping.

(MOHAN *has now moved forward towards* DEVLIN *and* BAJORIA, *his eyes fixed on the American.*)

MOHAN: That's a spaceship, Mr Devlin.

(BAJORIA *swivels round toward* MOHAN.)

BAJORIA: What? Whashship?

(MOHAN *ignores him. Suddenly* DEVLIN *turns to* BAJORIA.)

DEVLIN: Hang on to this!

(*He hands over the gun to* BAJORIA *before he can protest, lunges forward and dives into the pond. A buzz rises from the crowd.*

175

MOHAN *watches tensely.* KALYANI *moves forwards to stand beside him, holding on to his arm.*

DEVLIN *makes his way through the lotuses and reaches the spaceship. He clambers up the curved side, finds the viewport, and is about to look inside when the spaceship suddenly begins to throb.* DEVLIN *dives back into the water and swims rapidly back to the shore. He climbs up the slope, stands panting and waves his hand at the capsule.*)

DEVLIN: You got the first live temple in history out there, Gug.

(*The red glow of the just-risen sun now pervades the lotus pond. An awe-struck silence sweeps over the crowd, and the bird noises are hushed too.*

It is DEVLIN *who breaks the spell.*)

Explosives! Singh, get the explosives!

(SINGH *and most of the other workers are in the crowd, and they make a dash toward the drilling site.*

DEVLIN *snatches the gun away from* BAJORIA's *hand and screams into his ears.*) Drive to the nearest phone booth – call the US Embassy – call the Army Headquarters – tell them to send help – it's an emergency – there's a spaceship here and it's a source of danger . . . GO!

BAJORIA: Danger . . . Hey Ram! . . . Hey Bhagwan!

(BAJORIA *bundles himself into the limousine followed by his entourage who seem as confused as he is.*

The panic spreads to the villagers who run about in confusion, leaving the immediate surroundings of DEVLIN, MOHAN *and his wife, and the dredging personnel.*

MOHAN, *white as a sheet, turns to* KALYANI.)

MOHAN: Get back home, for heaven's sake!

KALYANI: Not as long as you're here.

(DEVLIN *has run up to the truck, and hauls out a stout wire rope with the help of the workers.*

BAJORIA's *car swerves round, but the chauffeur has lost his nerve too and runs the car into a tree.*

A light – the same light that we saw dimming in the first scene – now begins to pulsate through the wall of the capsule, and a strange musical hum like a drone begins, and over this drone begins the song. This is HABA's *song, sung in a strange, metallic, unearthly voice. The song brings the crowd trickling back to the pond. Everybody turns to the spaceship, now bathed in the light of the sun, and still emitting its own strange light which pulsates to the rhythm of the song.*

EXT. BAMBOO GROVE. DAY
HABA's GRANDMA *has come out of her shack and is looking around.*
GRANDMA: Haba, where are you? Where have you been all this time?

INT. CABIN OF SPACESHIP. DAY
Inside the spaceship, the ALIEN *sits crosslegged on the floor in the classical manner of the Buddha, a red disc of sunlight on his face and around his head, singing the simple song about flowers and rivers and paddy-fields that* HABA *has taught him.*

Around the ALIEN, *in this gravityless cabin of the spaceship, float* HABA, *in a state of blissful slumber, and the various specimens of earthly flora and fauna he has helped to collect for his 'friend' – a frog, a firefly, a snake, a lotus, a squirrel, a* bulbul *bird – all in a state of suspended animation.*

The ALIEN *now stops singing and stretches his hand towards an invisible control.*

EXT. LOTUS POND SURROUNDINGS. DAY
The spaceship begins to rise slowly out of the water. It rises until all the submerged portion comes into view, so that it now floats on the surface of the pond, and everybody can see and recognize its form, that of a child's humming top. The throbbing has now increased in volume and frequency. Suddenly, the viewport of the capsule, now seen clearly, flashes redly as it catches the sun.

DEVLIN, *crouching with the gun, shouts as he sees the flash.*
DEVLIN: Get down everyone, dive under cover!
    (*Himself rolling into cover,* DEVLIN *aims at the window and fires a burst of shots at it.*)

INT. CABIN OF SPACESHIP. DAY
Inside the spaceship, unperturbed by all the external commotion, the ALIEN *stretches his hand towards another control.*

EXT. LOTUS POND SURROUNDINGS. DAY
There is a sudden hissing sound, and the spaceship is enveloped in a

greenish vapour, the hum glides up to a dizzy pitch, and with a sound like that of a high-C pizzicato on a hundred violins, the spaceship blurs and vanishes.

The vapour spreads over the pond; the lotuses all droop and wither; the flowers vanish, and the paddy goes back to its original state.

DEVLIN *is the first to find speech.*

DEVLIN: Jesus!

> (*He slumps down on the grass, still dripping from his swim, unnerved, exhausted and yet elated by his experience. He turns to* MOHAN *and grins.*)

Well, I guess you can go write that story now!

> (MOHAN, *still in a trance, smiles back.*)

MOHAN: As soon as I've found the words.

> (KALYANI, *white as a sheet, but relieved, happy and proud, rests her tired head on her husband's shoulder.*
>
> DEVLIN *now turns to* BAJORIA, *who is sitting on the grass, his legs stretched out, a glassy look in his eyes, and his lips curled up in an idiot smile.*)

DEVLIN: You still want the water pumped out, Gug?

> (BAJORIA *raises his hands and starts to clap robot-like, and begins to hum his favourite* bhajan.)

BAJORIA: Papapapa pum papa pump pump pump

papumpa pum papa pump pump pump . . .

> (*The clapping now extends to the crowd, but this is not to keep time to* BAJORIA's *singing, but to applaud* DEVLIN. DEVLIN *turns to the crowd, puzzled. All eyes are turned on him.* BOSE *turns to* PRAMANICK.)

BOSE: It's all in what you get to eat, really. I'm sure there's no adulteration in America.

> (DEVLIN *turns to* MOHAN *for enlightenment.*)

DEVLIN: What the hell's going on?

> (MOHAN *smiles.*)

MOHAN: That's for you. They're cheering you.

DEVLIN: Me? Why?

MOHAN: They think you've saved them.

DEVLIN: *Saved* them?

MOHAN: From the Alien's magic. They were not too happy about the miracles.

> (*The cheering is now deafening.* DEVLIN *gets up and throws up his hands.*)

DEVLIN: Holy smoke!
    (*He turns to* BAJORIA, *who is still clapping and singing.*)
    You see what you've got me into, Gug. I'm a comic book
    hero . . . a goddamned *Superman!* – Oh boy oh boy!
    (DEVLIN *starts walking, past the pond, away from the crowd,
    his body shaken by a wild, uncontrollable laughter at the monu-
    mental absurdity of his predicament. The gun in his hand is the
    only absurdity he can do something about; he takes a look at it
    and flings it into the pond. It descends on a bunch of broad lotus
    leaves, causing a startled frog to jump clear. Then it slithers off
    the leaves and sinks into the pond.*)

The Chess Players: script conference with Satyajit Ray

GLOSSARY

Baba   An honorific used by holy men; a holy man.

bhajan   A semi-classical Hindu devotional song found all over India and often sung in groups accompanied by instruments like the harmonium.

bhang   Indian hemp used as a narcotic and intoxicant.

Brahmin   The highest of the traditional divisions of Hindu society, considered to be descendants of Brahma, the creator of the universe. All Hindu priests are Brahmins.

Chamar   A low caste throughout India whose occupation is tanning skins.

chillum   The part of a hookah which contains the tobacco and charcoal balls; (loosely) a pipe.

dhoti   About six metres of cloth wrapped around the lower half of the body in various styles by males in north India.

durbar   A court or public levée of an Indian prince, or, later, of a Governor or Viceroy under British rule.

ghazal   A sung couplet, the second line of which must end in a rhyme. Amorous in character but at times containing matters of a mystical nature, it is the most popular form of Persian and Urdu poetry.

Gond   An ancient tribal group distributed all over central India.

Kathak   A north Indian style of dancing, characterized by fast footwork and interplay of rhythms, performed by both men and women. It was influenced by both Hindu and Mughal traditions.

lota   A metal pot.

paan   A mildly addictive preparation of areca-nut, catechu, lime paste, and other condiments wrapped in a leaf of the betel tree, chewed all over India, especially as a digestive after meals.

raga   One of sets of scales and melodies used as a basis for improvisation in Indian classical music.

Santhals   A tribe scattered all over Bengal, Bihar and Orissa, renowned for the beauty and independence of their women, and the eroticism of their love songs and poetry.

shehnai   The classical wind instrument of north India, a favourite in temples and especially at weddings.

thumri   A style of singing that developed out of earlier classical styles at Lucknow and Benares. Its name derived from 'thumuk', the sound of a graceful stamp of the foot. It has always been associated with dance and with arousing the erotic sensation.

NOTES

The following sources are among those consulted in the writing of the introductions to the screenplays, in addition to personal interviews with Satyajit Ray, Lindsay Anderson, Saeed Jaffrey and Shama Zaidi.

p. 3   Interview with. V. S. Naipaul by Andrew Robinson, *Illustrated Weekly of India*, Bombay, 5–11 July 1987, pp. 8–15

Ray, Satyajit, *Jakhan Choto Chilam (When I Was Small)*, Calcutta, Ananda Pubs, 1982 (memoir of his early life)

p. 5   Khanna Rajbans, *Illustrated Weekly of India*, Bombay, 22 October 1978, pp. 49–53 (review of *The Chess Players*)

Ray, Satyajit, *Illustrated Weekly of India*, Bombay, 31 December 1978, pp. 49–53 (Ray's reply)

Sharar, Abdul Halim Sharar, *Lucknow: the Last Phase of an Oriental Culture*, E. S. Harcourt and Fakhir Hussain trans., London, Elek, 1975

p. 9   Seton, Marie, *Satyajit Ray: Portrait of a Director*, London, Dobson, 1978, p. 165 (quotes Ray's letter to Chandragupta)

p. 12   Radford, Tim, *Guardian*, London, 18 January 1979

Canby, Vincent, *New York Times*, 17 May 1978

Interview with Ray by Iqbal Masud, *Satyajit Ray: Retrospective Souvenir: The Second Decade*, Swapan Majumdar ed., Calcutta, 1979, pp. 23–4, 26

p. 77   Mahmood, Hameeduddin, *Screen*, Bombay, 18 June 1982

Vohra, Bikram, *Sunday Observer*, Bombay, 7 October 1984

p. 122   Watson, Francis and Hallam Tennyson, *Talking of Gandhi*, Bombay, Sangam Books, 1976, p. 89

p. 122   Ray, Satyajit, 'Ordeals of the Alien', *Statesman*, Calcutta, October, 1980

p. 125   Clarke, Arthur C., *The Times*, London, 24 August 1984 (letter)

Interview with Ray by Sumit Mitra, *India Today*, New Delhi, 15 February 1983, p. 51
p. 125 Caulfield, Deborah, *Los Angeles Times*, 16 March 1983